Streets of Conflict

Streets of Conflict

Michael Anthony

Ian Randle Publishers
Kingston ● *Miami*

Published in Jamaica, 2007 by
Ian Randle Publishers
11 Cunningham Avenue
Box 686
Kingston 6
www.ianrandlepublishers.com

© Michael Anthony

ISBN 976-637-288-8

A catalogue record for this book is available from the National Library of Jamaica

First published by André Deutsch Limited in 1976

Cover and book design by Ian Randle Publishers

Printed in the United States of America

To Carlos

Every country has its troubles, and Brazil is no exception. In mid-1968 a wave of student riots hit Rio de Janeiro. Although this novel is based on those riots, in no intention whatsoever to criticise the Brazilian regime.

1

Craig leaned against the railings of Vista Chineza, looking down at the city. But he was thinking neither of Rio de Janeiro nor of the wild, hectic Carnival that ended last night. His mind was on Marisa. He was wondering if Mac was really going to bring her along today.

He felt a bit tired and he yawned. The city of Rio de Janeiro lay far below, and the drop made him dizzy. Only yesterday he was down there in its very heart – in noisy bewildering *Centro*. He tried to pin-point *Centro* now but he could not. He knew it was somewhere before him down there, but he did not know exactly where it was.

He said to himself: 'Boy, that was a crazy Carnival!'

Although he was thinking of the gay, streaming mass of people, his mind still centred on Marisa. Without knowing why, he thought he had never met a person so strange and fascinating. He had met her yesterday, in the crowd, but she had not even seemed a part of that crowd. He had been with his friend Mac, and Mac had called out to this girl, and they had stood up on the oavement talking. She had looked so serene that she had not even seemed aware of the din about her.

He looked at his watch. It was only half-past ten. He had to get down to Praça Saens Pena for twelve noon. There was no problem in finding Praça Saens Pena, he knew where it was. He was only hoping that Mac would keep his word and bring Marisa along.

He told himself: 'Let's see what sort of man Mac is.'

He looked down at the city again. Rio de Janeiro lay like a picture postcard, with the blue waters of Guanabara Bay as a background to the skyscrapers and to the green of the trees and the white strips of beach. There were countless islands offshore.

His thoughts shifted to his uncle. The uncle never expected to be in a place like this. So far as travel was concerned, Brazil could not have been further from his thoughts. Had his uncle not found himself here, he, Craig, would never have seen anything of these parts. Yet, in many ways, Brazil was so much like home. Despite the Portuguese language. Take Marisa, for instance, he thought. For what she looked like, he could have met her anywhere in Trinidad.

He looked at his watch again. It was creeping on to eleven. Maybe he'd better take his time and go and dress and go down to meet Mac.

Mac, he thought and shook his head. Like his uncle, Mac, too, was a puzzle. He was not able to understand exactly why Mac came to this country. And the story about his having a school of English – well, he would see today. He hoped it was true and he also hoped that it was true that Marisa was a teacher of his. This would make things easier!

His heart began racing a little. Although the time was not quite eleven he felt he had better go and get ready. Praça Saens Pena was only a half-hour journey away, down the hill, and he did not have to get there until noon. But he was growing a little anxious.

He turned from the railings of Vista Chineza and started walking back along the Rua da Boa Vista. The rarefied air of Alto da Boa Vista made him feel a little cold. He walked down the busy high street, beside shops and some decrepit buildings until he came to Rua Ferreira de Almeida, on his right. He turned and walked up it. The street rose steeply and ran up to the foot of a towering peak. Where the road ended, on his right, was his uncle's house, or rather, the house where his uncle lived. It was the last house on the street, and the peaks of the *serras* rose sheerly beside it. He could never understand what made his uncle choose Brazil, in the first place, and in the second, what made him come to the very top of the Rio heights.

2

When Craig arrived at Praça Saens Pena it was not yet noon. Mac had arranged to meet him in the praça so he went there and sat down on a bench, waiting. Around him were a lot of wooden benches under big trees, and there were diagonal paved walks converging on the centre of the praça. In the centre itself there was a big totem pole with Carnival decorations hanging from it. And all around on the ground were bits of coloured streamers and paper and old masks and dominoes and other evidence of the Carnival.

From where he was he could see a clock at the far end across the street and he had about ten minutes to wait. He had no idea whether Mac and the girl, would arrive together, or whether they would meet here separately, and he did not know what direction they would come from. He realised, from Marisa's conversation yesterday, that she lived near by, and now he was looking all around the praça and he told himself he did not care from what direction she came – once she came.

Not too far from him was a big pear-shaped pool and there was a hose spouting up water into the air and the water was falling on the other side, forming an arch. He sat looking at this and looking around at the things in the praça. This place, from the bus, always appeared to be a hive of activity, but now on Ash Wednesday it was quiet. The Carnival must have half-killed everybody, he smiled to himself. There were only about three or four other people sitting on the benches.

The sun was blasting down but he was sitting in the shade of the trees. Now, after the coolness of Alto da Boa Vista, there was the sensation of the air shimmering with heat. Perspiration was beginning to form along the sides of his face.

He looked at the clock again and now he got up and started scanning the place. He walked around a little and then he stood up by the side of the pool and began looking around the praça again.

The place seemed to be growing livelier. There were a few people walking through, crossing from the street on one side to the street on the opposite side, and there were a few children playing in what looked like an entertainment park. This was at the lower end.

Looking at the clock Craig saw that the hands had slipped past the hour of noon. Now he was impatient. He walked right down to the end of the praça where the children were. There were swings down there, and a slide, and a merry-go-round, and a see-saw. He went past the playground and down to the pavement and looked to both sides to see if he could spot Mac. The big clock was right there in front of him now and the time had just turned five past twelve. The street here was littered with coloured paper blown about by the wind, and at times, when the wind was high, the paper bothered the motorists. Just in front of him was a triangle of road that linked the two major streets passing beside the praça.

He stood there a little while, looking around, and he noticed it was getting on towards a quarter past twelve. He began feeling dejected because it did not look as though Marisa and Mac would turn up. He went back to the side of the pool and as he looked to see if any new people were walking into the praça, a quiet voice said: 'Hello, Mr Craig.'

Craig turned round. 'Hello Senhorita Marisa!' he said, his heart pounding.

She said, That is right.' Then she started speaking in Portuguese and he raised his hand: 'If you can, speak English, please. My Portuguese is not good today.'

She laughed. 'This is good for me because I like the English. You come now here to meet Mac?'

'Yes. He asked me to be here at twelve o'clock.'

'He asked too for me to come at twelve. He wants to show you the school?'

'Yes. He said so. But it doesn't look as if he's coming.'

'Mac, he is always late.'

Marisa turned, looking up the Rua Conde de Bonfim to see if there was any sign of Mac. As she turned, Craig looked at her stealthily. His heart was still thumping. He said: 'He's coming from up there?'

'Yes, his house is not far that way.'

'And I just came down that road.'

'Yes. That way is from the Alto da Boa Vista.'

'I live up there.'

'Mac, he told me.'

Craig did not know how to assess this girl. She seemed completely unaware of how attractive she was. At the same time, she seemed, like yesterday, very friendly and vivacious, but in a way, very distant.

There was a little silence, then she said, 'You enjoyed the Rio Carnival?'

'Very much.'

'It is like the Carnival of Trinidad, no?'

'Well, yes and no. You see, Carnival is Carnival, so it's similar. But they are very different. You see—'

She said: 'Mac he said the one in Trinidad is better.'

She was looking at him. He did not know what to say and he did not want to commit himself. Eventually he said: "Mac said so? I don't know. It's hard to tell which is better. I like the one here very much.'

'Thank you, I am glad. But it does not matter if you prefer the other one.'

'No, I really enjoyed the Rio Carnival.'

'I am glad,' she said. 'But not always I like the Carnival.'

Craig looked at her, not knowing what to reply. Marisa looked around the praça then turned her head towards the Rua Conde de Bonfim. The sun was very bright and she shaded her eyes with her hand. Silently Craig looked at her and he felt overwhelmed. He told himself he had never seen such a wonderful black girl. As she turned back to him he pretended he was looking at the buildings around. She said: 'Mac said you are staying with an uncle here?'

'Yes, I have an uncle up at Alto da Boa Vista. I am staying there. He is a bit lonely, you know.'

'He is from Trinidad?' She asked, puzzled.

'Yes, of course. My uncle had a little – well he had a little wife trouble, and he just rushed away and came to Brazil. Funny, eh? He just came here just like that. He just disappeared from Trinidad and we had a letter from him from here in Brazil.'

'Oh,' Marisa said. Then she was silent. She looked serious and thoughtful and she turned her head towards the upper Rua Conde de Bonfim. Craig himself was thoughtful for a while, but then he left off thinking of his uncle, and as he glanced at Marisa again he could feel his heart thumping in his chest. He did not know how to start a conversation that could lead to anything. He thought of her there beside him, so elegant and attractive, and he wondered if she had any idea of how he felt. To break the silence he said: 'You live near by?'

'Yes. Right down there in the Rua General Roca.' She pointed to the street running crosswise in front of them.

'Since yesterday I wanted to ask you about your English. It's so fluent. I think Mac said something about your coming from America?'

'That is true. I was born in America but my father and mother are Brazilians. My father used to work on a ship and then he stayed in Nova York for many years.'

'And you speak English at home?'

'We speak English at home.'

'That's why.'

There was a long silence, with both of them looking to see if Mac was coming. Then Craig said: 'My uncle said he went to Manaus first.'

'Manaus! That is a long way. Far to the north. That is in Amazonas.'

'I think there was some company there recruiting workers for a railway or something. An English company and they wanted English-speaking workers. A lot of people went from the West Indies.'

She did not quite follow but she nodded her head.

Craig said: 'He said he couldn't take the life there. Too much bush and hard work. So he came here to Rio instead of going back home.'

'He is here a long time? In the Rio?'

'Five years.' Then he chuckled: 'But he doesn't speak any Portuguese.'

'Five years and he does not speak the Portuguese? *Nossa Senhora!*' Marisa could hardly believe it. She knew Craig was not joking, but she found that his uncle being here five years and not being able to speak any Portuguese was next to impossible. She was about to speak when Craig said: 'Look up there – up the hill. Isn't that Mac coming there?'

Marisa looked up the Rua Conde de Bonfim. 'Yes, Mac is coming. It is Mac.'

Mac walked down the pavement, crossed the street, then trotted to the praça, towards them.

3

As soon as Mac joined them, Marisa said, 'I am sorry, Mac, but I cannot go with you to the school. I came only to tell you that I have to go out with my father today.'

Craig's heart sank and he felt deceived.

Mac said: 'But you didn't know that before?'

'No, it is my father. And also, you are very late.'

Mac said: 'Hell. This is Ash Wednesday. What's the matter with you? Because you born in America you have to be punctual? This is Brazil. Anyway, what happen? You have to go out *now* or later?'

'He is already waiting for me.'

Mac looked resigned. He said: 'Anyway, you remember Craig – from yesterday. He's only in Rio for a little time but afterwards he might well come back and be one of our teachers. That's why I asked you to come. For us to show him round the school. He said he'd like to see the school.'

'Yes. This is very good.'

'But you have to go now.'

'Yes. I must go.'

'Anyway, next time.' He turned to Craig: 'As you see Marisa ain't have much of a problem with English. In fact she ain't have none at all. She could talk it just as she could talk Portuguese. So you know, anything that crop up, it's up to you.' He was going to make a quick wink but Marisa's eyes were on him. He said to Marisa: 'Leave it to me. I'll show Craig round the school.'

'Okay then. *Ciao!*'

As she turned to go, Mac said: 'By the way, I nearly forgot. I'm inviting Craig home on Sunday. We'd like you to come.'

'For your house?'

'Yes. Linda told me to ask you. You doing anything special on Sunday?'

She put her hands to her forehead. 'The Sunday *que vem?*'

'Yes. Sunday coming.'

'I will come.'

'Okay. Good girl. I'll tell Linda.'

She had already turned away, when she came hurrying back. 'Mac, you did not tell me what time.'

'About half past twelve so.'

'Okay. That is all right.'

'Fine. Thanks a lot. We'll look out for you, eh? *Ciao!*

Ciao!'

She hurried out of the praça by the path that led to the Rua General Roca.

When Marisa disappeared down the road, Mac said: 'I don't feel she's going anywhere with her father at all. She just didn't expect to meet you here and she fix that up right away. Those girls so damn smart. You see, we was supposed to be going over there to make the place ready for the reopening, but seeing you she got smart, boy.'

'I don't think she'll come on Sunday.'

'Oh, she'll come all right. If Marisa say she'll come she'll come.'

'That's a lovely black girl, eh?'

'You could say that agian.'

'You sure she ain't have no boy-friend, Mac?'

'I didn't say she ain't have no boy-friend. I don't know. But what I said yesterday was, I said she didn't seem to me to have any feller now. But I couldn't say, really. Chaps does fall for Marisa like fly for molasses. But she ain't easy, if you see what I mean. She's really, a hell of a nice girl.'

'She's a girl to keep any man in Brazil.'

'Well perhaps you'll stay in Brazil, who knows. Don't mind I'm laughing but I'm serious, you know. Anyway, you notice how much I'm backing you up? You talked so much after you see the girl yesterday, well you'll have a chance to chat her down on Sunday. You'll hardly meet another *Carioca* as cute as Marisa and who could talk English. I mean a black girl.'

Craig did not say anything for a while. Then he said: 'She seems crazy about English.'

'Everybody in Brazil is crazy about English. Everybody find English *bacana*. You know what *bacana* is? It means "special," "fabulous," that sort of thing. That's one of the slangs here. When you learn Portuguese and talk to these girls you'll see how they'll throw themselves on you to learn English without paying.'

'They'll pay all right.'

Mac laughed. 'That's what you think! You don't know Brazilian girls, boy. Okay, you'll find out for yourself.'

'If Marisa was so cagey today I don't see how she'll come on Sunday.'

'If Marisa say she'll come, she'll come. That's one *Carioca* who's reliable.'

'What's *Carioca* again?'

'Oh, that's anybody belonging to Rio.'

'I see.' Then he said: 'Well anyway tell me how to find your place because I'm coming on Sunday.'

'Okay, but you want to come and have a look at the school now?'

'It far from here?'

Mac chuckled. 'No, just here, man. Across the road there. You could see it from the praça.'

'I'd really like to have a look at it.'

'Well let's go across,'

The Instituto McWilliams de Idiomas was just in front of them when they crossed the road. Hanging from the eaves of the building was the signboard of the school, and under it was a stairway that led up to the classrooms. They climbed the stairway, and then there was the reception room, and beyond it the three large classrooms of the school.

The walls of the classrooms were plastered with educational charts and pictures, and the furniture consisted of modern desk-chair combinations, and there was audio-visual equipment. Craig said: 'But you really have something here, man.'

'You like it? If you come back to Brazil this is yours to teach in. I would really like somebody like you here. Somebody who really knows English.'

'But Marisa is good.'

'Well, she's damn good but you can't say English is her first language. And I could do with another teacher anyway. It's like hell to get teachers here and everybody wants to learn English.'

'I might take up your offer, you know.'

'But I want you to take it up. I'm doing everything for you to take it up.'

Craig said to himself: 'I'd give anything to come back to this town. But I don't know.' His mind was filled with Marisa.

Mac said: 'Walk around good and see what the little place is like.'

Although Craig did not say very much he was surprised to find the place looking so smart and up-to-date. At least it looked like a flourishing concern. It was the sort of place he did not mind coming back to.

Mac said: 'Take a good look around. It's not much really. Walk all over the shop.'

4

When Craig visited Mac's place on the Sunday afternoon Marisa was already there. The three of them – Marisa, Mac's wife, Linda, and Mac, had been sitting in the verandah conversing in Portuguese, and when Craig joined them Mac and Marisa changed to English for his benefit.

Craig realised this and said: 'No, carry on. Keep on talking Portuguese. I'm all right.'

Mac and Marisa were amused. Mac said: 'But this funny, eh? He can't speak Portuguese and Linda can't speak English.' He said to Craig: 'By the way, you ain't meet Linda yet – my wife.'

Mac spoke to Linda in Portuguese and she got up and she and Craig shook hands.

Afterwards Mac said: 'Perhaps you'll make it quick, boy. I mean this Portuguese business. The language ain't so hard. And I'm sure with *the* sort of approach you have you'll be rattling off Portuguese just now. And if you stay here, you in the right country for it. With Linda, now, it's like hell,' he chuckled. 'We living together for two years but she's still so dumb about English. Boy, this girl slow to pick up!'

Linda looked at them and now, as they smiled, she smiled too. This made Craig feel like laughing out.

Marisa said: 'But for Linda it is not so bad, really. Because it is only two years. The uncle of Craig, I can't believe. He is in Brazil for five years, and he still can't speak – yes?' She looked at Craig.

Craig said: 'That's right.'

She laughed. Craig looked across at her face and his heart was thumping because of the closeness of her.

Mac said: 'But that old man – he is a special case, boy.'

Craig said: 'But even so, Marisa is unusual. She's good. Her English is perfect.

'Perfect. No,' Marisa said, 'But I am trying always to speak the

English well.'

Mac said: 'I told you Marisa was born in America? This girl speaking English from the time she could talk. And they speak English in the house, too. Her house. I mean, you have to give her the credit for keeping up the language, but again, I know Marisa, so I'm not surprised. English is an obsession with this girl,' he laughed. 'I like that.'

Marisa said: 'You like that? Good. Because it is my whole life.'

'It is more than your whole damn life,' Mac said.

Marisa erupted in delicate laughter.

Craig noticed the closeness of the relationship between Mac and Marisa and there was just a tinge of jealousy and he tried to forget it because it did not seem to make any sense. Linda, on the other hand, was used to these two, and she did not entertain even a shadow of suspicion. Now, she did not understand a word of what they were saying, and she only kept looking from face to face and kept smiling with them. Marisa looked towards her now and gave her a brief summary of what the conversation was about and as Craig saw them chattering in Portuguese he was trying to understand what they were saying. Mac, seeing the two girls talking, turned to Craig.

'So how you finding Rio so far?'

'Rio looks like a nice place. I like it – but I don't know. The thing is, the language—'

'I know what you mean. Without the language you can't get the feel of the real place. I know exactly what you mean, boy, because I passed through that.'

'But apart from this, I think I like here.'

'Boy, Rio is a hell of a nice place. A true *cidade maravilhosa*, as they say in the song. That means, "marvellous city". And the trees and so on – the vegetation – it's like ours. And the people nice, too. But it have some things that would upset you. That is, if you is the sort of man like me. Anyway....'

Mac was talking but Craig was only half-listening to him now. His thoughts had drifted and he was thinking now of Marisa.

He was wondering what sort of girl she really was. She seemed ready to accept him as a friend – no doubt because of Mac. Although she looked the sober, dignified type, she smiled easily. He wondered if, as the afternoon wore on, he would get in conversation with her.

He suddenly became aware of Mac talking to him and now his mind came back to the moment and he shook his head in agreement with what Mac was saying, although he was not sure what he was agreeing to. He said to Mac: 'That's true, boy.' Afterwards his eyes were attracted by a big road junction near by, and he said: 'Rio busy, eh?'

Mac said: 'That junction is Uruguaia. You ain't see nothing yet. Rio is a hell of a place. You yourself saw yesterday what *Centro* is like. You think this is Port of Spain! Port of Spain is a little village compared to here.'

'I know.'

'Rio alone has more people than the West Indies.'

Craig thought a little and he said: 'Yes, that's true.'

Marisa heard that and she said: 'More people than the Trinidad?'

Mac said: 'More people than the whole West Indies – not just Trinidad. Rio has four million people.'

Marisa looked towards Craig. Craig said: 'That's true, because the British West Indies only have three million.'

'British you saying? 'Mac said.

'Well, you know what I mean. English-speaking, you know.'

Marisa looked surprised. She said: 'It is a small country.' She smiled at Craig and his heart raced.

He looked away slightly and his eyes caught Linda's face. At the back of his mind he did not want to get too excited about Marisa, at this stage. He looked at Linda and her face seemed very young to him. Mac had said almost nothing about her. He felt he knew why. He noticed there were no little children about and he turned to Mac: 'You ain't have no children yet?'

'No, not yet.' Mac tried to look sad but he did not seem extremely sorry that he had no children yet. He added: 'We only married the other day, you know. Not even two years yet.'

Marisa whispered to Craig: 'Mac, he is terrible. The Linda is only eighteen. She came down to Rio from Bahia and she went to study the English at the school of Mac. But he would not leave her alone!'

Craig laughed.

Linda knew that they were talking about her and now Marisa turned to her and in Portuguese explained what she had said. Linda laughed, and Marisa turned to Mac, teasing him. Craig felt a quiet wave of jealousy. He looked at her. Every word she said, every action she made, fascinated him. She seemed to speak both languages with ease, and in addition to that she seemed full of charm and elegance. And a quiet stylishness. Linda, beside her, did not attract his attention very much. He was a little curious about her because she was white, and because she was the only one of the company who did not speak English. Of course, *he* was the only one there who did not speak any Portuguese. But he had an excuse. He had just arrived in Brazil.

Mac broke into his thoughts: 'You hungry?'

'Just a little bit.'

Mac looked at his watch and looked back into the room. Someone like a maid was inside laying the table. Mac said: 'Boy, I hungry like hell. I didn't know it was one o'clock already.' He asked Marisa: '*You* hungry?'

She smiled but did not say anything.

Mac said: 'You shame to say you hungry? Well, stay there!' He said something in Portuguese and Linda got up and went into the house.

It was a hot day and the sun was blindingly bright on the road outside. The road was the same Rua Conde da Bonfim that ran up from Praça Saens Pena, and on the right it wound far up the hill to Alto da Boa Vista. There were a lot of people on either pavement, and although it was a Sunday there was much traffic. Mac noticed Craig looking out into the road and he said: 'You find this place like home, boy.'

'A lot. Not so much the place itself, but the people.'

'Really, in many ways here is just like home.'

Craig said: 'I was so ignorant about Brazil. I never knew this place had so much black people.'

'This is a surprise for everybody.'

Although they were not talking to Marisa she was paying attention and now she said: 'But why surprise? The Brazil had slavery too.'

Mac said: 'Yes, it's true. But we just talking facts, that's all. Nobody just ain't know anything about Brazil.'

Marisa said: 'I know, and it is terrible.'

Craig looked at her. 'I know when it comes to Trinidad people don't know anything at all about here. They know the country exists, but that's all. For instance, they don't even know what the language is here. Everybody thinks the language here is Spanish.'

They all three laughed.

Marisa said: 'But you say in Trinidad nobody knows about the Brazil, but your uncle, he came here.'

Mac said: 'Well, that's why. Because he didn't know.' There was laughter from Mac and Craig but Marisa still looked puzzled.

As Mac was going to speak, Linda came back. As she did not know what was going on she just sat down and stared from face to face blankly. Mac asked her something in Portuguese and she nodded her head. After a few moments the maid came and spoke to her, and Mac said: 'Okay, let's get up and go and eat something.'

As Mac was going in he threw his arms about Craig's shoulders and said: 'This country is nice, you can't deny that. It's nice in lots of ways But it have poverty like hell, too.' He looked sharply at Craig. 'And the hurtful thing is that the poorest people are the people like you and me.'

Craig did not say anything, and Marisa who was just behind did not say anything either. They went and sat down at the table. Marisa looked at the richly-stocked table and she could not help thinking about what Mac had just said. The table was oblong and Mac and Linda sat at the ends and Marisa sat in the middle facing Craig.

Craig looked towards Mac and said: 'What you said there about poverty is true, you know. Here has it bad. There was so many beggars around the place during the Carnival. That is one thing you don't see nowadays even in Trinidad.'

Mac said: 'You talking about poverty? You ain't see nothing yet. You ain't see the *favelas*, for instance. What we call *favelas* here. Shanty towns.'

Marisa was looking at them. Craig saw her and said hastily: 'I'm not criticising your country, you know. Because I'm only a stranger. But I was a little surprised, to tell the honest truth. This is a nice shining, beautiful city but I was a little surprised to see so many beggars.'

Marisa turned to Mac: 'Beggars?'

'*Mendigos.*'

Marisa said: 'Oh, beggars, yes. That is true of the Brazil – everywhere in the Brazil. But it is such a good country that Mac likes it so much that still he is here in eight years. I know it is bad, this poverty, but everywhere there is poverty too. And in the Brazil everybody has a chance not to be poor. Everybody has a chance.'

Mac stopped eating for a moment. There was still a lot of food on the table. There was a lot of rice and beans and meat and there were bottles of Brazilian wine and jars of fruit juice.

Mac said: 'You said *chance* – is *chance* you said? Which chance? The poor man have a chance here?'

Marisa kept looking towards Craig. 'Everybody here has a chance. I have a chance, Mac have a chance. And we are not rich. Even you who just came to the Rio – you have a chance here.'

Mac shook his head. 'All the Brazilians talk like that – black and white. And this does surprise me because they know better. They know this is fibs. For instance, a girl like Marisa shouldn't be teaching in my silly little school. This girl should be in university. I know what I'm telling you. This so-called equality here is a myth.'

Marisa interrupted: 'I am not saying that—'

'Just give me a chance. The thing is, Craig, as you see, Marisa is not *the favela* type. Her father worked in America for years, and *she* had a – well, she had a reasonable schooling. And she could speak *English*. Knowing English in Brazil is a hell of a lot. And yet, what happen? As a black girl I suppose she is doing well, and perhaps that's good enough for her. But it's not good enough for *me*.'

Both Marisa and Craig were silent. Mac went on: 'And looks count a hell of a lot, too. Marisa is an attractive girl. Doors will open to her that won't open to others.'

Marisa opened her eyes wide. Mac said: 'This is not flattery. But looks is not the point now. So take it cool.'

Craig was very thoughtful. With everybody silent now, he said: 'I didn't know things were like this here. Seeing the Carnival, with everybody mixing up, I thought things was different.'

'You'll learn fast,' Mac said.

Marisa was growing more and more uneasy. She said now: 'I am not saying that here we do not have any problem. But don't let

Mac to poison your mind.' She was looking towards Craig. 'I know what Mac wants is revolution. I don't want to see the Brazil in revolution. Revolution is the favourite word of Mac. We – how you say it – we argue all the time and I know. If people are happy, like in the Brazil, Mac is unhappy.'

Mac let out a big 'Stupes'. He said: 'You hear her? Boy I can't argue with her. If she could call one-tenth of these people "happy" then she ain't talking my language.' He got up and sat down again and he was so irritated that he stopped eating entirely.

There was a long moment of silence. Linda was looking at them and she knew that things had not been going well. She had been listening to see what she could pick up from the conversation but she had long given that up. Now she sat back and she was looking around the table. She lifted her eyebrows questioningly at Mac but he did not even see her.

Mac was still thinking of what Marisa had said about people being happy and about what he wanted was revolution. He was still very incensed about that. Marisa did not want revolution but there was bound to be revolution in Brazil. A bloody revolution! He breathed hard, then he calmed down. After a few moments he noticed that no one was in a mood to talk. To break the silence he said to Craig: 'You enjoyed the Carnival yesterday?'

'Oh yes. And Monday too.'

Marisa asked him: 'It is like the Carnival of Trinidad – yes?'

'It's like the Carnival in Trinidad. I mean with everybody jumping and dancing in the streets. It's the same sort of mood, you know. But I feel as if the steelbands in Trinidad make so much difference.' He looked at Mac. 'She knows about steelbands?'

'Not really.'

Craig said: 'Anyway, I like the Carnival here. It's different but I like it.'

Marisa translated this to Linda and Linda beamed and looked very pleased. Marisa herself was thrilled. She said: 'You heard about our Carnival already – there in Trinidad?'

Before Craig could answer, Mac said: '*Claro*. Rio Carnival is famous.'

Marisa said that to Linda in Portuguese and Linda was excited and wanted to hear more. They had all finished eating and Mac noticed the maid waiting to take the dishes away. He said: 'Let's move to the front.'

Out in the verandah conversation came easily. They talked a great deal about Rio's Carnival and about Rio itself. They talked in English most of the time but on occasions Mac and Marisa talked in Portuguese for Linda's benefit. Many times when Mac and Craig were talking Mac wanted to touch on what he called the false side of Brazil, but he did not, for not wanting to upset Marisa.

Marisa sensed what was going on in Mac's mind. It was because she knew Mac so very well. She knew when he spoke sincerely and when he did not. When he talked about Brazil without criticizing it she knew he was not being sincere.

At the moment she was paying more attention to Craig. She found him quiet and gentle and he was very much the sort of person she liked talking to. And of course, he spoke English, which was really what mattered to her. And he did not seem to be obsessed with politics, like Mac. He was nice and comfortable to talk to and she very quickly felt at ease with him.

Craig was quick to spot this. He wanted to capitalise on it but he did not wish to seem too anxious – though he did not want to be too slow. He talked about the Carnival and about the places he had seen around Rio, but when Linda followed Mac to the kitchen, he said: 'Where exactly you live, Marisa?'

'In the Rua General Roca.'

His heart was racing. 'And you teach in Mac's school?'

'Yes. It is near by.'

'Mac is lucky,' he said. He could hear his heart hammering inside him.

'He is lucky? Why?'

There was a pause, then Craig said: 'You are a beautiful woman.'

Marisa laughed. She had realised, of course, that Craig was interested in her. This was not a new experience because every day she met someone who was interested in her. Sometimes this sort of thing irritated her and sometimes it amused her. She was amused now, and in a way, flattered, not only because she thought Craig an innocent, naive, boy, but because she liked him too, though in a different way. She liked the sort of person he was and she liked the fact that he spoke English. She could not dream of having an affair with him because in the first place he was too young for her, and in the second, he was only a bird of passage, as it were. She wondered how old he was but she did not ask him. She said: 'You are only in Rio for a while?'

'Well, at the moment it's just for a short time. But after I go back to Trinidad I'll come here for good.'

'You hope to come back?' she said surprised.

'I'm coming back to live here.'

'You like Rio so much?'

'I like other things in Rio so much.' And he gave her a meaningful look.

She chuckled and smothered the laughter as Mac came back into the verandah.

Mac said: 'So you two going all right?'

Marisa looked at him as though she did not understand. Craig said: 'I wish I could speak Portuguese like how this girl could rattle off English.'

'You making joke, boy. You just come to Rio. Don't worry about the language, you'll learn it – it ain't hard.'

Linda came into the verandah with coffee and when they settled down again Craig said: 'You said Portuguese isn't hard, but what about my uncle. I was telling you about him. He's here whole five years and he can't say anything in Portuguese.'

Marisa couldn't help laughing. Mac chuckled: 'Your uncle is a special case, boy. Sounds to me like a hell of a case. He couldn't be trying, really. I mean, he might be trying *not* to learn it. These things happen sometimes, you know. Psychological.'

Marisa was still very much amused. 'He is old? How old?'

'Only in his fifties.'

Mac said: 'In any case age ain't nothing. Once you collective, and you hearing a language all the time, you *bound* to learn it. Your uncle sounds like a special case. It's really odd. Now, take my wife – take Linda – it's like hell for her to learn English, because she doesn't hear enough English. Though if she was keen—'

Linda interrupted: 'Wife, yes, me.' They all laughed. Mac told her what he was saying and she nodded and said: 'Me no speakee English yet.' They almost choked with laughter.

The four of them sat in the verandah conversing cheerfully until

the shadows from the mountainside stretched long towards them.
The tops of the mountain peaks were in bright sunlight. Far away
and high over the city Craig could see the statue of Christ.

'Look the statue of Christ.'

Without looking up, Mac said: 'Yes, boy. Famous statue.'

Marisa did not say anything.

Mac said: 'That is *Christo Redemptor* – that's how we call it.
You could see it from almost every point in Rio. *Christo Redemptor*
means Christ the Redeemer. I call it Christ above the *Favelas*. It's a
very appropriate name.'

Marisa listened to him but they did not look at each other. Mac
said to Craig: 'You know what *favela* is? Just cast your eyes a little
lower down those mountains. You see all those rows of shacks up
there? That's the *favelas*.'

Neither Marisa nor Craig spoke. Mac was looking at Craig.
'*Favelas* is the Portuguese word for slums. All around Rio you could
see them. They call them *morros* sometimes. It's mainly black people
who live in those shacks and I don't care who vex but these are the
people who concern me.' He seemed worked up and his face was
taut but he tried to appear calm.

He said: 'Everytime I see that statue up there I think of the
favelas. Because what the statue say is this: it is saying that since
these people have Christ they don't need anything else. And they
don't get anything else, anyway. Make no mistake, these are the
bastards who suffering.'

Mac paused but nobody spoke. Craig glanced towards Marisa.
Marisa was looking out into the street and she was wearing the look
of one determined to be unruffled. After some moments of silence,
she said: 'Mac, it is time for me to go. I must to leave now.'

'You *must to leave now* or you *must leave now*.'

'I am sorry. You know more English.'

'No – *I* am sorry. You teach in *my* school.'

Marisa smiled wryly.

Mac said: 'But to be serious, don't forget tomorrow is back to
normal. Classes as usual, eh?'

'Yes.'

Marisa got up and she said something in Portuguese to Linda
and they both went inside the house.

Mac said to Craig now: 'You reaching her down to the praça – down to Saens Pena.'

'I want to do that.'

'You want to do that! You *must do* that. This is your big chance.'

'We'll see. You think it's worth it?'

'Of course it's worth it, you ain't have eyes or what? Marisa is a treasure, boy. Not only for what she looks like, but for what she is. Don't mind us, you know. We quarrel a lot but we still the best of friends. We don't agree at all, and this is because, well, politics. Anyway, you dam' lucky, because things in your favour.'

'Things in my favour? You find so?'

'Only a blind man can't see that the girl have a little soft spot for you.'

Craig felt excited. Mac said: 'That's one thing with Brazil, boy. It's a hell of a place but it's nice. And when you meet a good girl you meet a good girl, I could tell you. You don't get a lot of them like—'

He saw the girls coming out and he stopped talking, and then he changed the conversation. When Marisa came out to the verandah he said: 'Craig will reach you down to the praça. From there he'll catch a bus back up to the Alto. It's easier from Saens Pena.'

'All right. Thank you,' Marisa said.

Craig and Marisa left the house and turned down along the Rua Conde de Bonfim. There were many other people walking along the pavement. The sun had already sunken behind the mountains at their back, and vehicles already had their sidelights on. Mac watched the two of them disappear in the gloom.

5

They walked side by side, Craig's heart thumping. He felt it was a wonderful opportunity walking alone with her and he wanted to say something to start a conversation, but he could not think of what to say. As they walked, she looked beside and up towards the shacks on the hills. Then she said: 'Trinidad does not have *favelas*, no?'

'Well, we have some. In fact, we had a place in Port of Spain that was just like your *favelas*.'

'Yes, I think they are in every poor country.'

'Of course.'

'Mac gets very angry to see the *favelas*.'

'Perhaps he sees this as a rich country and he thinks they shouldn't be here.'

'It is true. He thinks the Brazil *should* be a rich country. He is right. The Brazil is big, and it has much – how do you say – *recursos minerais?*'

'Sounds like "mineral resources".'

'That is true. It has a lot of that. But we have now to develop.' She shrugged her shoulders. 'It takes time. What can we do?'

'Mac might hate the *favelas* but on the whole he loves Brazil. Don't worry. In any case, Brazil is not all *favelas*. So far as I can see Mac really loves this place.'

She did not answer at once, but after a while she said: 'Sometimes I think so too but he is always talking against it. He says there is bound to be revolution here.'

Craig did not reply to this. He was thinking more of her than of what she was saying. And of course he did not want to talk politics. He said: 'So you are American?'

She smiled. 'Me? I was born in Nova York so for this I am American. But I don't so much want.' She looked at him. 'I prefer to be Brazil.'

The way she said this amused him and he laughed. 'And I am

Trinidad,' he said.

'*Claro.*'

They came to the big intersection of the Rua Uruguai and they crossed it and continued walking down the Rua Conde de Bonfim. They fell into silence. She noticed him glancing at her but she was very discreet and pretended not to see. They walked side by side and for a while the only sounds were of their own footsteps and the footsteps of the other people walking down to the praça. And of course there was the noise of the passing vehicles.

He said to her: 'But you aren't saying anything.'

'You too are not saying anything.'

'And suppose I say something!'

'Yes, please.'

His heart was racing again. He said: 'I only spend two weeks in this place but you are really a lovely girl.'

She laughed.

'This is the truth. I'm talking my mind.'

She said nothing. She was thinking of him and what she regarded as his folly. She liked him but not in the way he wished. But she could not tell him that. At least, not yet. She remembered his story about his uncle on Alto da Boa Vista, and she thought: Craig, too, will suffer much. It is perhaps in the blood. She said now: 'Your uncle, it is very strange, no? It is sad.'

'I don't even like to talk about it. That was a big shock to us. The man just left Trinidad and went away.'

'And now that he sees you he will go back or he will stay here?'

'He won't go back. He'll never go back. He said so himself. There's certain people he doesn't want to see ever again in life. No, he won't go back; he'll stay right here. As a matter of fact, when I say that I'll come back, I'm planning to stay with him.'

Craig said this last not only because it was on his mind but also because he wanted to clear any doubts from Marisa's head. He knew that he would not have a chance with her if he gave the impression that he was going away for good. The more he thought about her it was the more he did not want to go away at all, and he was now thinking more seriously about returning.

Marisa was at the moment occupied with avoiding the little depressions on the pavement. The dusk had fallen heavily now and she could not see very well. The street lights were quite dim. They were walking slightly downhill and there were great trees at intervals on the pavement, and occasionally they crossed little side streets. She continued walking carefully in the stiletto-heeled shoes. Craig's hand was close beside hers and she would have taken it, were Craig not inclined to be so amorous. Why were men so silly? Why did they always have to indulge in the love game? Why couldn't they be just nice friends, sometimes?

There were quite a few people walking down the street now. The lights of the roadside houses reflected on the pavement, and some little children, fascinated, were jumping and skipping. She looked at them. The nearer they themselves drew to Saens Pena the greater the number of people on the pavement became, and at this time they were in almost a crowd. Craig kept walking very close to Marisa and now and again their hands knocked together and everytime this happened his heart beat fast. He wanted to take her hand and she knew it and she chuckled in the dark. Now, apart from the steady stream of light from the vehicles going up the Rua Conde de Bonfim they saw headlights swirling round and round in a huge circle, which meant they were almost at the praça. In the distance, reflecting against the trees were the coloured lights of the totem pole.

When Craig saw Praça Saens Pena he realised that he had little time remaining with Marisa and he said now: 'I'd like to – to at least meet you again.' His heart thumped so loudly he could hear it.

'Why not? We can meet again.'

'When?'

'Anytime – when I am not teaching.'

Craig felt a surge of relief. Now he felt confident that she liked him. He said: 'Well, how we'll see and when?'

'I do not know. Perhaps you want to see the Rio. There are many places interesting for you. I could go with you and show you much of the Rio.'

'That will be fine. I'll be so glad.'

'*Claro,*' she said. She was smiling at him and she looked very calm and serene.

'What's "*claro*"?'

'Oh, I am sorry. It is one of our expressions. It means, "of course".'

Praça Saens Pena was now just in front of them on their right, and they crossed the street and walked down beside the big Banco da Guanabara at the corner. In front of them was the Rua General Roca which cut across the Rua Conde de Bonfim. There were many people about and on the other side the praça itself was teeming with people. In the dusk they could not see much of the Carnival decorations over there, but the lights of the totem pole showed up flags and buntings between the trees. Marisa had slowed down in front of the Banco da Guanabara and Craig said: 'You crossing over to the square?'

'Oh no. I have to go home.'

'And from here, where you live?'

'This street. This is Rua General Roca. At the other end.'

'Well I'll walk—'

'No, it is fine. It is all right.'

Craig felt very disappointed. 'So you don't want my company?'

'I like your company but we'll meet again.'

He was quietly excited. 'You said you'll show me around Rio.'

'Oh yes. I forgot that. When we go we could get on a bus and I will show you the places.'

'When? Tomorrow?'

'Tomorrow, no.' She considered a little and said: 'Really, the best is the end of the week. We have more time.'

Standing there she looked a little impatient and Craig realised that she wanted to leave. He was still feeling disappointed and he thought her very strange. He wondered if she really liked him, as he had thought. Just looking at her and being with her she had grown in him and now he felt he wanted her more than anything else. He felt the weekend was too long a time away but in any case he decided to take what he could get. He said: 'What about Saturday — you could make the trip on Saturday?'

'Trip?'

'I mean if you could go out with me on Saturday and show me Rio.'

'*Claro*. Saturday is good. We could take a bus from the praça, over there, and go right down to the Copacabana. It is a very interesting drive.'

'I'm dying to go out for a drive with you.'

She chuckled. Under the street light he looked down at her smile and at her glinting teeth. He said to himself: 'Oh God, this woman nice!'

She said: 'Okay, then. I must go now.'

'But we'll meet on Saturday?'

'*Claro.*'

'Right here by this bank, eh? Right here in front of this bank.'

'What hours – what time?'

'Goodness me, I nearly forgot. What time you could come?'

She thought a little and she said: 'Four o'clock – yes?'

'Yes, that suits me. Anytime suits me. I'll be right here.'

'Yes. Well I will go now.' She stretched out her hand to him. Then she said: 'Your bus for the Alto da Boa Vista. You see that big cinema over there? The Olinda? You go over there and catch it.'

'Oh yes. Okay.'

'I see you on Saturday. *Até logo!* We say "*até logo*" for "goodbye".'

'Oh, I see. *Até logo,* then. Please don't forget, eh?'

'Oh no.' She turned and went down the street.

6

Craig walked over to the bus stop in front of the Olinda Cinema, but as the bus for Alto da Boa Vista was some time in coming he crossed over into Praça Saens Pena.

The praça was brightly lit and teeming with people. Although there seemed to be nothing in particular going on here, the people were milling about and there were many sitting on benches, talking.

There were many children in the praça and their noises were everywhere. Some were running and playing in the part where he was and he could see other children on swings in what looked like a playground far to his right. Above, the brightly-coloured lights of the totem pole made the centre of the praça look like a wonderland.

He said to himself: 'These people like they still having their Carnival!'

He ambled slowly along, looking about him. Between the paved pathways the place itself was very green with low-cut grass and shrubbery, and there were also many flower-beds. The pathways themselves were very wide and converged on the centre of the praça, and there were benches all along their edges.

He walked through and across to the side where ran the Rua Conde de Bonfim. Here, there was a sort of fountain, with a jet of water spouting from one side of a pool to the other. There was nothing more about the fountain except the jet of water spouting.

He stood up, trying to take Marisa's face from his mind. He looked back to the centre of the praça where there were crowds of people moving in all directions. People seemed to be pouring into and out of the praça and outside on its pavement there were crowds who seemed to be continually circling it.

He thought: 'I wonder if she'll come, really.'

He looked up at the lights and at the fluttering buntings and at the other Carnival decorations. Above, there was not a star in the sky. The air felt heavy. He was aware of the loud drone of the chatter about him, but as he knew no Portuguese at all he did not even listen. There were a few people who looked as though they wanted to talk to him but he did not want to go through the trouble of making signs to show that he did not speak Portuguese. So he avoided them. He walked around the fountain and then he went out onto the pavement of the Rua Conde de Bonfim. Then he turned left and ambled up to where the praça ended. He turned left again, into the Rua General Roca, and when he came to the other end of the railings, the Olinda Cinema was across the road to his right. He crossed and went to the bus stop.

7

It was drizzling when Craig arrived at Alto da Boa Vista, and he had to make a dash for home from the junction to avoid getting soaked. When he arrived home his uncle was dozing away in an armchair. The uncle looked round and said: 'Opa! Boy, you come?'

Craig was breathless.

The uncle looked at his face and clothes. He said: 'I didn't realise rain falling.'

'It just start. It coming down even heavier now.'

'Well, so help me! I sitting down here and I didn't know.'

The uncle got up and stretched his long body. Then he went to the windows but he had already shut them all. He looked out towards the street. The rain was already beginning to pelt down, and it was making a noise against the concrete steps and against the street. The uncle sat down again. He said: 'Well, this is something. In February Rio don't see rain at all. It should do the ground good.'

Craig stood up in the centre of the room. His hands were on his hips and he was still panting from having run up the street in the rain. He said: 'It should do the ground good but it will do me bad. If this sort of thing continue all week it's real trouble. I have to go out with somebody Saturday.'

'Oh yes. Is that girl you was telling me about? You meet her?'

'Yep.'

'And what about the Trinidadian feller — you see him too?'

'It was his house we went to.' Craig walked over to the bedroom to change his clothes.

'Oh, I see. And you chat with the girl and thing? What he say?'

'Who?'

'The Trinidad feller.'

Craig was in his room and now they had to raise their voices because of the noise of the rain.

'Unc, this girl is not his girl, you know. Mac is a married man with a wife.'

'Oh, I see. Trinidadian wife?'

'No. Brazilian. A white Brazilian. She can't speak any English at all.'

'Is so? And how they does talk? He learn any Portuguese?'

'*If* he know Portuguese? That man does talk the language like a native. If you hear him you'll think he's Brazilian.'

'Well I wouldn't know because I don't speak this damn language.'

Craig came out now and sat down on a chair in a corner of the room. The uncle was not far from him. Craig was now in clean, dry, clothes and feeling good.

The uncle said: 'And how long he here, this Trinidad boy?'

'I don't know. I think it's five or six years. Like you. But when you is a young man the langauge come easy.'

'Oh, he's a young feller?'

'Yes, only about twenty-eight so.'

'Anyway, I can't stand this damn language and I don't talk it.'

Craig smiled. After a moment he said: 'But this teacher girl — you know I told you that Mac has a school in Saens Pena. Well, she's teaching English there. Uncle, this girl is really something. She's Brazilian, but she's fluent in English like you and me. Mind you, she was born in America, but she came here small and she spent all her life in Brazil.'

'Her parents is American or what?'

'No, that's the thing. Her father used to work on some American ship — I can't remember — and at one time he was staying in New York. He learned English too, over there. They does talk it at home.'

'Oh, well that's why she could talk English so good. That's nice, though'.

'But Uncle, if you see the girl! A real black beauty. And she has education and refinement to go with it. She's fantastic'.

'All right, all right. Don't forget you only here for three months.'

Craig did not say anything. His face looked all excited.

'You hear me?' The uncle said. 'You could like this girl if you like but don't forget you only here for three months. Don't get mixed up in any Brazilian callalloo.

Craig just smiled. The question of coming back was on his mind but he did not want to touch on it now. In the silence he became aware of the tumult on the roof above.

He said: 'This rain wouldn't pass.'

'Boy, don't worry about the rain. Let the rain fall.'

'Oh, I forgot you like rain.'

'Always.'

'But I want next Saturday to be nice.'

'Well today is only Sunday.'

Craig was lost in thought. The uncle looked at him then looked at the rain beating down on the glass window beside him, He was feeling cosy and nice and he was happy because the rain was falling. For it meant that the young plants in his garden would get a good drenching. Not that he did not water them during these dry, hot days, but pipe water was not the same as rain water. What was falling was their own sort of water, he thought. He looked very content.

Planting was his passion. Since he arrived in Rio it was the only thing he gave himself to, completely. It was the only thing he did in his spare time to keep the depression off his mind. Here he planted everything he could lay his hands on, and the little plot around the house was green with bodi, and pigeon peas, and ochroes, tomatoes, melongenes, and all sorts of garden vegetables. He never learned the Brazilian names for them. As he thought of the kitchen garden now, and some of the things he had got from it to cook today, he said: 'But wait – boy, you ain't hungry?'

'Not really. Not at this moment.'

'What happen? What you have on your mind?'

'Nothing really.'

'You look like you thinking far.'

'Is so?'

Craig's thoughts were very mixed up. He was thinking of what would be a good excuse to return to Brazil, because he knew that once he got back to Port of Spain it wouldn't be so easy. He was thinking of this, and he was thinking of Marisa, and he was thinking of the rains not passing. Then his thoughts slid to Praça Saens Pena and he was wondering what the rains had done to that crowd. It must have scattered the crowd in the first few minutes, leaving the place desolate and bleak. Leaving the coloured lights of the totem pole shining against the trees and the grass. Leaving the fountain and leaving the swings of the playground lonely and wet in the night.

He yawned. Only a while ago he was down there and you could not stick a pin in the praça, so crowded it was. Now everybody there was certainly chased home from the rain. And chased into the restaurants and the coffee shops and against the eaves of the buildings. Marisa was at home. What was she doing? He imagined he was talking to her and there was a half-smile on his face.

The uncle said: 'You smiling to yourself, boy. You happy?'

'Me? Happy? I so tired.'

'Then why you don't eat and go inside and rest.'

As Craig looked at his uncle's face now his mind ran straight on his mother. Perhaps this resemblance to his mother was the reason why this uncle was his favourite. This could be only part of the reason, he thought. For all through the years — especially the school years — this man had been right by his side, encouraging him, helping him at every turn. The only sad thing was that Charlotte. Auntie Charlotte. He called her 'Auntie' but he never liked her. This man had been far too soft for her.

His mind remained on his uncle's wife, and as always when he thought of her, anger welled up in him. She had led his uncle a hard life, and he, Craig, had almost got used to that. But he could have hardly believed it when, at this stage of their lives, she left him for another man. Yet, that in itself was not all. It might have been a blessing in disguise. But the really painful part of it was his uncle's reaction. It was madness. It was nothing short of madness to abandon everything and run away.

This was a sensitive point and Craig would not touch on it now. He simply said: 'But Uncle, you mean you just living to yourself like that? You don't go out at all — you don't even go to the pictures?'

'Me? What I going to the pictures for? I don't talk the language so what I want there?'

'That's true. Though they have English pictures here.'

The uncle was mumbling. Then he said: 'Boy, you don't know how I does catch hell! I does catch hell at work and all.'

'Yes? How?'

'I is the only one in the bunch who does speak English. Everybody else talking Portuguese.'

'And you can't even try and learn a little bit of the language, Unc.'

'I know a little bit but I don't talk it. I does understand.'

'But how come you got this job?'

'Well the firm is an English cigarette firm. You doesn't see Wightman do Brasil when you pass down by Usina? From the time the boss hear me talk English, he said: "You is my man".'

'That was lucky.'

After a little silence the uncle turned to him: 'Look, I think you better have something to eat now, boy. Okay?'

'All right.'

The uncle got up and went into the kitchen. Craig was not really hungry. It was drizzling heavier outside and he listened to the water falling and he said to himself: 'Oh God, I only hope this weather take it easy this week. I don't want weather like this for Saturday.' He was thinking of going out with Marisa.

The uncle said something from the kitchen. Craig could not hear because of the rain and he got up and went to the kitchen door. 'What's that, Unc?'

'I said you must bring up the Trinidadian boy some time. And his wife, too. And that new girl-friend of yours.'

'Good. Okay. I know Mac will be glad to come.'

'Yes, and even after you gone back he could still come. So, you know, I'll have somebody to talk some old talk with, sometimes.'

'Sure. Fine. I'll bring him.'

The uncle stopped what he was doing and said: 'Boy, you know how it is to hear somebody talk English in this place! Sometimes I don't hear English for months.'

'I realise that. I could well imagine.' And then he said, 'If it's somebody you want to talk English with, what about me — because I might come back.'

The uncle stopped and turned around. He said: 'You thinking of coming back?'

'I might.'

'Really? I mean, you want to come back here — to live? That's a damn good idea, but what will your mother say? In any case, you feel you like the country enough?' The uncle's face seemed all alive.

'Sure, I like Brazil. I like Brazil a lot. From what I could see already, I don't mind living in this place.'

'It's not that teacher girl who turning your head!'

'Oh, no, Uncle. A big man like me!'

'Anyway this is a business you have to study because it's your whole life in front of you. If you make it back here you wouldn't be like me — you young — you'll learn the language quick. As you know, I come to this country just by chance, but I think it's a good country. At least with your education you should make good.'

Craig went back to the front room. The uncle seemed a lot brisker and he was quickly laying the table and afterwards Craig went and sat at the table to eat. He was sitting facing the road and looking outside. It was still raining. The sky looked black and heavy and the air was full of mist, and the high mountains on the other side of Alto da Boa Vista were one with the night.

The uncle went in, and when he came out again he was in his pyjamas. Craig had his supper and afterwards he went out into the kitchen with the plate, and the uncle called out to him: 'Leave it there like that.' When Craig came back out of the kitchen he went and sat at the table again and he cupped his face in his hands and yawned.

The uncle said: 'Boy, you better go in to your bed, yes. Get up, get up.'

The little house had just two bedrooms. From the living room in which they were sitting, a corridor led to the bedrooms. On the right of the corridor was the bathroom, and on the left was the first small bedroom and then the big one. Craig got up and went into the small bedroom.

8

It rained all week. When Craig got up on Saturday morning the uncle had already left for work and he found himself alone in the house. The first thing he did was to look at the weather, and he was relieved to see that the rain had stopped. But the skies were dark. He spent the morning trying to read Brazilian newspapers, but every now and then he glanced up at the skies. Far from clearing, they became more and more overcast. Now, towards midday, a fine drizzle began coming down.

He felt very dejected. He stood up at the window looking outside anxiously. The window beside his bed opened out towards sheer mountains in front of him, and against the mountains Craig could see the fine, slanting drizzle turning more and more into a shower. Thick, grey mist was sliding down the mountainside, and where there were trees, the mist was creeping out like smoke from among the leaves.

'Stupes!' he said.

He opened the window and put his hand outside to see how hard the rain was really falling. As soon as he opened it a gust of wind blew rain and mist into his face and he was forced to shut the window quickly. He said to himself: 'Christ, this blasted rain coming down, boy!'

He sat down again, trying to read the Brazilian newspapers, but he was a little unsettled and his mind was flitting to all sorts of things. And all the while he was conscious of the rain outside and was listening for it to stop. Of course, Marisa was right on the surface of his mind and now he tried to forget her a little by making an effort to understand the words before him.

He thought the language tough and impossible to work out. Although he recognised a word or two, this did not get him very far, and his eyes soon became tired, and he dozed off right there on the chair.

When he opened his eyes again it was half-past two. His heart thumped. It was getting on to the time for him to go down to Praça Saens Pena to meet Marisa. He was planning to leave at about half-past three and give himself plenty of time to arrive at Praça Saens Pena for four o'clock. The only thing to upset his plans was the rain, which was hammering down. He looked outside. Then, depressed, he went into the small bedroom and sat down on the bed.

After a few minutes he got up and went out into the living room and looked out towards the bottom of the hill. Inside the house it was so dark that he switched on the light. The sky was slate-black and the high mountains on the other side of Alto da Boa Vista were hardly visible for the weather. The rain was beating down fiercely against the streets and against the houses. In the distance above the roof-tops the forests looked like cloud.

He felt trapped. The house beside him had all its windows and jalousies closed. The house was lying on much lower ground because of the steep slant of the hill, and he could see the water skirting off its roof in sheets. The houses on the other side of the street were all shut up too and this made the place look dismal and deserted. He moved over to the part facing the street, and with the rains appearing to blow in only slightly, he put his head out and looked down the street. Down to the point where Rua Ferreira de Almeida swung away from view there was nothing in sight but the mist and the rains blasting on the pitch. Just before him in the road, little streams were already rushing down the hill.

He said: 'Just the day rain shouldn't fall water pelting down like mad!' He made another stupes and sat down heavily in a chair. He mumbled: 'Even if this stupid shower stop now it's no use. Jeesan Christ!'

He looked at the old alarm clock which was on the safe in the living room and he saw that it was a quarter to three now. He still felt determined to go down to Praça Saens Pena. Although he could not imagine Marisa turning up in this weather he told himself he would make it even if he had to swim.

He got up again and went and looked out. He was wearing a rather thin round-necked jersey, and he felt the chill of the day and he shivered a little. There was no sign of a break in the weather and before him in the street now the mist was thick and low and seemed to be rolling down the hill.

He went in and threw himself on his bed and he stayed there for a little while. There was a little noise in his stomach from time to time which reminded him that he had not eaten anything since he had had breakfast. There was a lot to eat in the house but he had had his mind so taken up with Marisa that he had not bothered. Now he thought of going and making a quick cup of cocoa to warm himself. But as he went out into the living room he saw that the clock-hands had moved on to ten past three and now he definitely had to start getting ready.

He went inside to dress. He did not intend putting on anything like a suit because he was sure that Marisa would not turn up. And it made no sense spoiling good clothes in this weather. He watched the rain beating against the glass window. He just had to try and make it to Praça Saens Pena because he was feeling so pent up that if he did not go he would be so miserable he would find it impossible to sleep. He just had to go.

He put on a pair of khaki trousers and a thick, round-necked pullover. He put on thick socks and a pair of plimsolls instead of leather shoes. There was no umbrella around nor did he have a hat and he did not know how he was going to face this weather, but he was going to face it. The bedroom had also a window that opened out onto the street but as he attempted to open it now cold rain whipped in on his face and he slammed it in hurriedly. He took up the newspaper and decided to use it as a shield for the rain and now he went out into the living room to the front door. He stood up a little and listened to the muffled roar of the weather outside — then he opened the front door and went out onto the steps. The wind and the rain lashed him violently. He locked the door quickly and fled down the street.

9

When Craig got down to Praça Saens Pena it was only twenty-five minutes to four. It was still pouring with rain. As the bus turned the corner by the Banco da Guanabara he looked out although he could not possibly have expected Marisa to be there. No one was there in the rain. There was no one even sheltering there because the buildings had no eaves. The bus splashed water onto the pavement as it took the other corner of the praça and came to a stop. The stop was just in front of the Olinda Cinema and he dashed out of the bus and ran straight to the cinema's entrance hall to shelter. He took out his handkerchief and wiped the wetness of his neck and face and hands, and looked around him.

There were only three other people in the cinema entrance hall sheltering from the rain. The place looked desolate but it appeared that a show was going on inside as there was a cashier girl in her little box office. One of the people sheltering was a shoe-shine man of the praça with his stand and his little box of equipment. The others were an old beggar and a little bare-footed boy.

Craig moved right up to the front of the cinema entrance hall, just avoiding getting sprinkled. He had seen the shoe-shine man look at his shoes and he did not intend to have his shoes cleaned to go out in this weather. The shoe-shine man was sitting on his box in the corner. As Craig glanced at him there was a slight tug on his sleeves and looking round he saw the beggar. Craig moved away to the other end.

Now he stepped slightly back towards the box office as the gusts blew in the rain. He was feeling a little uneasy about these people behind him. Looking across at Praça Saens. Pena itself he could not see a soul. The massive, brightly-painted totem pole looked dull and washed-out in the rain, and all the trees looked grey and shrivelled up, and the playground part of the praça with the swings and see-saws and merry-go-rounds, looked abandoned and deserted. From where he was standing he could not see the Banco da

Guanabara because of the trees, but even so he looked in that direction. Afterwards he began looking at the bus stop right across the praça, for he was already thinking of how to get over there to catch the bus to go back.

He was quite certain now that Marisa was not coming.

He felt a bit disappointed although he had told himself that he could not expect her in that weather. The vehicles which were passing near were spurting water onto the pavement and he moved back a bit. Some of the buses, half-empty stopped, at the bus stop in front of him.

He was feeling a little uncomfortable because of his clothes. As he had run down Rua Ferreira de Almeida in the rain he was feeling dampness all over his body. He was not drenched but he was wet. Neither his hard-wearing khaki trousers nor the kind of pullover he was wearing absorbed water. As he looked down at his clothes he felt another tug.

It was the little boy who was begging. Craig was going to chase the boy away but as he looked round he saw that the girl in the boxoffice was looking at him. He pushed his hand in his pocket and gave the boy a note. He did not even look at the note well to see the value of it because he knew these notes were almost worthless. He felt revolted that such a little boy should be begging. He thought he'd better move off before the shoe-shine man came next.

The shower had now declined to a heavy drizzle. Craig looked to his left where he knew there were restaurants. Perhaps it would be better to go there, he thought. He looked round and saw the shoe-shine man looking at him. He dashed out into the rain.

A few doors along was one of the big, usually noisy restaurants of the praça, but it was now dismal and empty. He stepped in for a little respite from the rains, and got out again quickly. He headed for the little coffee shop at the corner — a shop he had spotted from the bus. The bleakness and wetness of the day, the absence of crowds from this normally busy part, and the disappointment over Marisa — all this combined to make him feel depressed. When he reached the coffee shop he took out his handkerchief and wiped his face and passed his hand over his head. Then he sat down on one of the high stools.

The man behind the counter said '*Chuva!*' and watched the

rain and shook his head. Craig did not understand but he smiled, and he ordered a cup of coffee.

There were quite a few people in the coffee shop, and their voices were raised because of the rains outside. He was looking not in the direction of the praça now, but towards Rua General Roca.

The street sign had a little notice underneath saying that Rua General Roca led to Maracanã, and as he sipped his coffee now and stared blankly into the rain he thought vaguely that one day he would go to Maracanã football stadium to watch the great Pele play football. At the back of his mind there was still Marisa and the disappointment of not seeing her, and he was wondering now whether this rain would ever cease so that he could run over to the other side of the praça and catch a bus home. It did not make any sense hanging around Praça Saens Pena in this rain. There were already sheets of water on the ground and the wheels of cars and buses were squirting jets of water onto the pavements. Now as he looked, there was someone coming up the Rua General Roca with an umbrella and a heavy raincoat. The person looked into the coffee shop, stopped suddenly, then walked up onto the pavement.

It was Marisa.

10

Craig said, 'Oh — Good God! Girl, it's you? You out in this rain?' He was astonished and wildly glad.

She said: 'I did not want to leave the house, but I am thinking *that* you are standing outside the banco waiting for me. You did not wish me to come?'

'Didn't *what*? You making joke! Girl I'm so happy. Come in here from the rain.'

Everyone in the coffee shop stopped talking and turned around listening to the English.

Craig said: 'You'll take a little coffee for this chilly weather?'

'No, no. Now I don't drink coffee.'

Craig was pleased. The people in the coffee shop were a boisterous, rough-looking group and he did not particularly want Marisa to remain here. He said: 'You want to go somewhere? You was telling me about a bus ride.'

'Yes, but in the rain it is not nice to see the Rio.'

'I don't mind. I'll still see a few things.' He did not have the courage to say that it was only she he really wanted to see.

He finished his cup of coffee and got down from the stool. Marisa was standing there looking elegant with her raincoat and her rain-hat and with her umbrella in her hand. There was silence in the coffee shop and all eyes were on these two.

Marisa said: 'Let me see what bus ride is the best we must take.' Then she bowed her head, thinking.

As she was considering Craig looked at her and his heart was thumping and he was feeling as though he had scored a great victory. Marisa was standing on the edge of the coffee shop floor with the pavement so that the water from her raincoat could drip outside. Her hat was a waterproof one, brown and oily-looking, made from something like snake-skin. It had a wide brim, and it was floppy and falling into her face. It was the first time he had seen her with something on her head and she looked like a black model.

She said: For a nice ride there is the 416 bus.'

'Oh, yes.'

'We catch that bus right here, by the Olinda.'

'Okay.'

She started to open out her umbrella to go out in the rain. Craig looked at her and smiled. He said: 'Girl, I'm looking at your "Everton Weekes" hat. You wouldn't know about Everton Weekes. It has to do with a game called cricket. No, I mean I like that kind of floppy style. You see what I'm talking about?'

She looked puzzled. 'No,' she said.

'Okay, one day I'll tell you about this sort of thing. You think we should go out now? This rain coming even harder.'

Without answering she stood looking out at the rain. He was on the edge of the pavement beside her and the rain blew in on them slightly. Now they were on the side of the coffee shop facing Praça Saens Pena and Marisa looked towards the upper side of the Rua Conde de Bonfim for any 416 bus that might be coming towards them. She said now: 'The 416 is good because it goes right down to the end of Copacabana — what we call the *Posto Seis*. The places it will pass is much beautiful and you will like it. It is not through the town but it is the old Rio, and Copacabana is the new Rio. *Posto Seis* is the end of the new Rio itself. To come back there is the 415 that pass through the city of Rio — which we call *Centro*. There is a very nice road called the "Aterro" and it' passes on almost the edge of the sea. *Bacana*. And then from the "Aterro" it goes through Praça Quinze, along the Avenida Presidente Vargas, and right back here and up to Usina. It is a very nice drive but you will be tired. I could stop out here but you go straight to the Usina and take a bus to Alto da Boa Vista.'

'No, I think I will stop out here.'

'It is easier for you to go up straight to the Usina.

'I'll drop out here to talk to you a little.'

She laughed: 'You will be so tired that you will not want to see me. This drive will take about two hours.' Then she said under her breath: *'Tanta chuva!'*

'What's that?'

She caught herself. 'Oh, I said in Portuguese "tanta chuva!" I was not thinking. It means "so much rain!" '

'Oh. "Chuva" is rain?'

'Yes.'

'I see.'

The rain was coming down a little heavier now and the street-sides were like little rivers and the water was being sucked noisily into the underground drains. The water was falling in large drops and every now and again a gust of wind would blow the rain into them and now they moved back a little further into the coffee shop. Behind them there was the rumble of conversation and Marisa knew it was about them. She only half-listened to the voices and now she really wanted to get away from here. Her eyes were fixed on the Rua Conde de Confim. All of a sudden she said: 'Look! Come, let us go, quick!'

There was a blue and white bus — a 416 — coming down. It stopped at the traffic lights by the Banco da Guanabara. Marisa opened out her umbrella and Craig paid for the coffee quickly. The man receiving the money said, 'Chank you,' and there was a peal of laughter. Marisa said *'Até logo,'* to them and they answered *'Até logo,'* as both she and Craig dashed through the rain to the bus stop.

The bus was half-empty and they sat down at the back, removed from everybody else. Craig's heart was racing. He wanted to hold Marisa's hand or do something like that but he was not quite sure of Marisa's feelings towards him. He decided to wait a little while. As the bus moved off Marisa turned to him and smiled: 'I am sorry. You cannot see any beauty of the Rio in this weather.'

'It's all right. Your beauty is enough.'

She laughed. Then she said: 'Me? I am not. But—' And she paused.

'But what?'

'Nada. Nothing,' she said.

They were both looking at each other. His heart was thumping and he was anxious to hear her say something to make him know that everything was all right. She, on the other hand, was quite composed. She liked him and wanted to be his good friend. Although she liked him mainly for his English, she also liked the kind of person he was and she did not entirely rule out that she could be in love with him. Now she just said: 'This town, it is very pretty. Often you see many things from the bus — the *Pão de Açucar* — which you call Sugar Loaf — the statue of Christ, and even the Guanabara Bay, but today it is too much mist.'

Craig did not take his eyes off her. He said: 'I don't mind. I don't mind the rain or anything. You can't have sun every day.'

She smiled. She had taken off the 'Everton Weekes' hat and exposed a head of beautiful, jet-black, plaited hair. Now she looked outside the window to see how far their bus had got to. After leaving Praça Saens Pena the bus had borne right and into the Rua Haddock Lobo and now it was about to turn south into the Rua Frei Caneca on its way to Copacabana. The skies were leaden grey, and although the torrential showers had held off a little, there was a great deal of mist and low cloud. As they were turning into the Rua Frei Caneca, Marisa said: 'That big rua there on the other side — it is the Avenida Presidente Vargas.'

'Oh, yes.'

'It is the other end of the Avenida Presidente Vargas, *sim*. During the Carnival time – when I saw you – you was at the beginning end of it. At the Candelária – the big church. You remember?'

'Yes,' he said. 'Rio is very confusing.'

'At first everywhere is confusing. This here now is the Rua Frei Caneca. It will take us to the Catumbi, another *bairro*. Then we are going to meet a long tunnel. When we come out of there the Rio gets very cool because you get the breeze from the sea. There it is Laranjeiras.'

'I like that name.'

'You like the name, yes? "Laranjeiras" means the orange trees – but that was a long time ago.'

'It used to be an orange estate?'

'Yes, but of that was a long time. When we leave the Laranjeiras we arrive in Botafogo and then in the Copacabana. I think the Rio is lovely. Always beside you there are the lovely hills.'

With lovely slums, Craig thought. But he did not say anything. Then he asked: 'How big is Rio – I mean, how many people?'

'Four million.'

'Four million! Oh yes, I think I heard Mac say that.'

She looked at the way he said that. 'You find it is much, or—'

'Girl, you kidding! That is more than the whole of the English-speaking West Indies put together.'

For a while she was not entirely understanding him, but afterwards she understood and she laughed. She said: 'And Trinidad – how is Trinidad?'

'It's only a little place. Compared to Brazil it's a joke, really.'

'It is a little place but it is big, no?' she smiled.

'You think so?'

'It is very big in name,' she said.

'Thanks. I think so too.'

It began drizzling lightly again. Now they were passing very close to the big hills which formed a backcloth to Rio and the shacks on the hillsides stood out plainly. Then the bus came to a cemetery, and after a while the tunnel of Reboucas lay straight ahead. Craig eased up close to Marisa and as he tried to take her hand she looked at him questioningly.

He said: 'Marisa, it's no point hiding anything. I have to talk plain. You know I'm interested in you.'

'And for that you wait for the Reboucas tunnel?'

'Me? No. I wasn't waiting for anything.'

He was going to say more but at that moment the bus entered the tunnel and it was suddenly dark. Dim lights went on in the tunnel. She looked at him and smiled but he could see only her white teeth in the dark. She was in a dilemma over him. She liked him but she did not feel that she was in love with him. She felt she wanted to be gentle without hurting him. She said now: 'Craig, I know what it is that is happening to you. Perhaps to me, too; I do not know. Today I am only showing you the Rio, yes?'

He was silent.

'You are a nice boy but I want to think about it. You are very young, and also you are going back to Trinidad.'

'Even if I have to go back to Trinidad I'll come back.'

'But you are going back?'

'Yes, but I'll come back.'

She did not look impressed. 'You are not sure.'

'I'm sure. I'm more or less sure.'

She smiled to herself. 'How many years – how old–'

'I'm nineteen now.'

She was taken aback. She knew he was young but she did not

expect to hear that he was nineteen. She was misled by the fact that he was tall. She said: 'You are really only a boy.'

'A boy? What's the matter with you. I finish college and everything.'

'You was at college?'

'Yes.' He did not tell her that he had done badly in the General Certificate examination. And that part of the reason he came to Brazil was to forget. She was looking at him and studying him.

He said: 'And you, Marisa – how old?'

'Twenty-one.'

'That's only two years.'

'That is only two years but I am a girl.'

Craig did not understand the logic of this but he did not say anything. They were sitting close up to each other but they could not see each other very well in the dark. Marisa guessed how badly Craig was feeling but she also knew that there could not be anything serious between them. She was trying very hard not to hurt him. She said: 'I am thinking about it and I will tell you. Okay?'

'Okay.'

They sat in silence. After what seemed a long while the bus emerged into the drizzle again and into the light of day. They looked at each other's faces and Marisa giggled. Craig smiled but inside he was feeling badly. Then he looked outside.

Here the place was very different. It was flat, and large buildings towered close to the road and there was the sea in the distance. Now, at intervals, the bell of the bus rang and people got out. Very few came in. Those who sat near to Marisa and Craig kept looking towards them because of the English. The bus, which was speeding in the direction of the sea, now came to a large fly-over and turned away behind some houses.

Marisa said: 'Here it is the Botafogo.'

'Botafogo?'

'Yes. Botafogo is famous. It is a seaside *bairro* of Rio and many famous people live here. Over on that side behind we have the Flamengo, and to the front it is Copacabana.'

'Copacabana! Now you talking. Everybody knows Copacabana.'

'I agree that it is the most famous place in Rio. Very soon we will be there.'

'Good. I can't go back to Trinidad without seeing Copacabana,' Craig said. He had recovered somewhat from his depression.

'They know the name in Trinidad?'

'What? Copacabana? Every single body know about Copacabana, girl. And they know of Brazilian coffee, and of course they know about Pele. Pele is the most famous.'

Marisa was thrilled to hear this. She just said: 'One day I go to Trinidad.'

'You want to go to Trin—'

'One day I go there but just to see the place.'

Marisa was chuckling. Craig said: 'Oh God, Marisa.' He took her hand now and she let him keep it. His heart pounded. She said: 'Why you say "Oh God"?'

'You *should* go to Trinidad. I want to encourage you to go to Trinidad.'

'I will go—'

'But to stay. It is a lovely place.'

'To stay? Oh no. You say it is a lovely place? *Claro*, it is a lovely place. You come from there and you like it. I like the Rio. Much, much. I don't think I will live anywhere else.'

'I don't mind living here, for you. I don't mind coming back.'

They looked at each other and the way he spoke, her heart pained her for him. He was still holding her hand – just because she did not want to take it away, but she felt she was beckoning him on to something futile.

He was only nineteen. She could never marry a man younger than herself – although now this was not the most important thing in her mind. She was questioning herself and the fact was that she was not in love with him really. And she did not want to be just playing a game, to be leading him on. She did not know what to say to him now so she just smiled and pretended to be happy. After a little while she saw the painted archway ahead of them, which meant they were entering Copacabana.

11

In Copacabana they travelled along the Rua Barata Ribeiro, which was lined with massive buildings and luxurious shops, and through every street that went off to the left there was a glimpse of the nearby sea.

The rain was still drizzling. There were not many people in the bus now and there was little or no talking. Craig was looking around at the grandeur that was Copacabana and he was truly impressed. There was a great number of people about despite the weather, and a lot of vehicles in the street. The bus ran along for quite a while and when it began to slow down it interrupted Marisa's thoughts.

She said: 'We are coming now to the *Posto Seis*. This is the end of the Copacabana.'

'So we get out?'

'Yes, *sim*. This is the end of the line. Now, you know what we do? We take the 415 and we go back through the city.'

'Okay.' He looked around him. 'I like here.'

'Oh, you like it? It is very grand and everything here is luxury.'

'It's great.'

When the bus eased up alongside the curb and stopped, Marisa and Craig hopped out quickly and they went to the eave of a shop to shelter from the drizzle. While sheltering, Marisa was very quiet.

'What are you thinking about so much,' Craig said.

'I was thinking about you and Trinidad. I cannot understand. If you have to go back why do you want to be in love with me?'

'But I said I would come back.'

'But this is not sense. This is too much trouble.'

'Not too much trouble for me. Only if it's too much trouble for you.'

She was silently thinking of a way to make him end his hopes once and for all. She said now: 'It is not that, because I like you very much.'

'Thank you. I promise—'

She interrupted him: 'Let's go across the road because the 415 is there. The rain, it will not pass today.'

'Okay. When you ready.' He wanted to take her hand but it was helping to press the raincoat round her neck. They waited for a break in the traffic.

From where they were standing the sea was close by, and there was an open view because the road had ended up in a big junction and there were no buildings in front of them. The coast, which had seemed to come in now swept away, forming a semi-circle, and in the distance on the right there were a number of buildings on the edge of the sea.

'Let us now cross,' Marisa said. There was a break in the traffic and they ran across the street.

They got on a 415 bus on the Avenida Copacabana and they sat down, not at the back this time but on the side seat that ran beside the driver. They could see more now ahead of them but now they were mostly silent because they were both tired.

They drove along the Avenida Copacabana, and except for the fact that the traffic moved in the opposite direction from that of the Rua Barata Ribeiro, this street was very much the same. One thing that made it different was that it was very much nearer to the sea. It was almost on the seaside and there were several glimpses of the beach. The beach was completely deserted today and the sea and the sky were one solid block of grey. There was nothing much to look out at.

Craig said: 'Oh, this rain.'

'There is too much rain. I am sorry.'

'Sorry for what? Don't be sorry. I'm enjoying it. It is a very nice outing.'

'I am glad you like it.'

Marisa had not taken her hat off her head and also her raincoat was buttoned up to the neck. Craig said: 'You cold?'

'It is cold.'

'But you not wet?'

'Some little.'

Although they were talking softly the people on the bus heard the English and began staring at them. The driver kept on glancing at them from time to time. After a while Marisa, feeling exhausted, leaned over onto Craig, and with his heart pounding he took her hand and he put his other arm across her shoulder. She did not say anything. He whispered: 'Don't fall asleep.'

'I will not fall asleep because of you.' They both laughed.

His head was near to hers and he had a burning desire to kiss her but he did not yield to the temptation. She herself said nothing. She did not like what she was doing now and she had become a little tense.

They travelled in silence for some time and it was not until Marisa felt a burst of speed that she opened her eyes and took note of what was around her. '*Aterro,*' she said. It was an opportunity for her to sit up and release herself from Craig's arms. She said: 'This part is Flamengo. Here is the *aterro,* and this road will take us to the city. You know *aterro? Aterro* is land that they put in the sea—'

'Reclaimed land.'

'Oh, yes. Reclaimed. Here it is reclaimed. Up to that line of houses over there, was sea.'

'Oh.'

Far to the left was the line of buildings that fringed the shore-line of the old Flamengo. There were many streets and much land between the *aterro* and the line of buildings, and on the right, the sea was about a quarter of a mile away, and in the space between there were parks and gardens. The bus travelled very fast and in a few minutes they were at the outskirts of the city, passing through a harbour and praça with some giant pillars. Here several roads converged and the traffic became intense and the bus just chugged along. Craig took Marisa's hand again and she was tense but she did not say anything.'

He said: 'How you call this part?'

'Here it is the Praça Quinze de Novembro. The big building out there in front is the Candelária church.'

'Candelária? I remember that name. I and Mac met you there for Carnival.'

'*Certo.* Right. It is the same place. You are surprised? The Rio is like that. We went right around and now very soon We will be on the Avenida Presidente Vargas again.'

Down the Avenida Presidente Vargas the Carnival decorations which had not yet been removed were wet and faded in the rain. The row of Carnival stands in the centre of the two broad lanes of the Avenida were just being dismantled and new wood lined the pavements of the street. There were not many people about now and the fine spray drifting across the road made the place look desolate.

Craig said, more to himself: 'And to think you couldn't stick a pin here for Carnival!'

'What's that?'

'I said you couldn't stick a pin. That's an expression we have in English.'

She smiled and told herself she must remember it. She had forgotten to ask him what it meant.

The bus was speeding away from the Avenida Presidente Vargas now and in a short while they were again on the Rua Haddock Lobo, and fast approaching Praça Saens Pena. Marisa was looking outside. Craig seeing that he was near journey's end, said: 'I think I'll come back to this country. What you say?'

'You want to come back here to the Rio?'

'Yes.' He turned to her. 'I'll come back for you.' He waited anxiously to hear what she had to say.

Marisa put her hands to her face: 'My honesty, I do not know.'

'You mean you honestly don't know – that's what you want to say?'

'*Sim.* Yes.'

'But I'm not coming back to try to take you to Trinidad, you know. I mean to live here.' His voice was trembling.

'Nobody could take me from the Brazil. I mean it. But I am sorry about you. Perhaps you can come back but I am not saying that you must come back for me.'

Craig was silently depressed.

Marisa said: 'When are you leaving?'

'Next month. The fifteenth.'

She translated 'the fifteenth' to herself, in Portuguese, and then she said: 'I will speak to you again before you leave. Okay?'

They were both silent.

Praça Saens Pena came in sight now and Craig said: 'I'll drop off with you at the square, then I'll take a bus up.'

'No, don't stay at the square in this rain weather. Go up straight to the Usina. There you will ask anyone to show you the buses for Alto da Boa Vista.'

'I already know the buses for Alto da Boa Vista. You don't want me to be with you a little?' His heart was paining him.

'I am sorry,' she smiled. 'The drive was so long. You are tired of me and I am tired too.'

'I? I could never be tired of you.' He said this with feeling but looking at her he could see she had really had a long day. She was looking away wearily. He sat still, thinking. After a few moments the bus ground to a stop on the side of the praça opposite the Olinda Cinema. Craig said: 'So you going?' He got up to make room for her.

She hesitated: 'It is better for me to go up to the Usina with you.'

He felt thrilled. She continued: 'You might not know the right bus for the Alto. There, it is confusing, no?'

'Very.'

'I will go up with you.'

When the bus had stopped at the praça most of the passengers had got off and now the bus continued almost empty up the hill. The clock at the praça was saying half-past four, but the weather brought on the gloom very heavily and there already were a few lights in the praça and in the restaurants and coffee shops around. It seemed to have continued to rain heavily here, for in the drizzle streams of water were running down the sides of the street.

Craig said: 'What a day, eh?' And he said to himself: 'I hope this isn't a sign for us.' He turned to her and he said: 'Girl, by the time you get back down here it will be dark and you'll have to walk home alone. Poor Marisa!'

She smiled tiredly. She was anxious for the bus to get to Usina and for her to see Craig off to Alto da Boa Vista, so that she could get down back to Praça Saens Pena and go home. Apart from the fact that she was feeling worn out, it was getting late. When they got to the big junction at Rua Uruguai Craig recognised it, but he did not recognise Mac's house. Marisa did not even think of Mac or of Mac's house. She was gripping her umbrella nervously and watching the thickening dusk. She was also wondering to herself what the relationship between herself and Craig would lead to. She had gone out with him, firstly to practice her English, and secondly to see if any strong friendship was worthwhile, but he was too young, and she would definitely rule out a love affair. She also wondered how genuine were Craig's feelings towards her. This was a man – or rather, a boy – on holiday, and when he left her to return to Trinidad, who knew if she would ever see him again? Who knew if he was talking about love only to have a nice time in Rio before going back? She was jerked from her thoughts by the line of shops that was Usina. The bus swung into a cobble-stoned square where there were buses facing all directions.

As the bus stopped and they alighted, she said: 'Your bus is over there on the far side. The green and white.'

'Thanks very much. It's okay. I'll find it.'

She still walked with him across the cobbled stones. Craig spoke, his voice thick with emotion: 'So Marisa, when I'll see you again.'

'You can see me at anytime. I teach from six to nine.'

'You wouldn't mind if I come down to Saens Pena on Monday, after your class. That's all right?'

She did not answer right away, and then she said: 'Okay.'

'Fine,' he said. He breathed out with relief. 'I'll be there waiting for you.'

He stepped into the bus for Alto da Boa Vista and he said 'Cheerio,' to Marisa, and Marisa replied 'Cheerio,' and she went off in the gloom.

12

The following Monday night Craig arrived at Praça Saens Pena at half past eight. The weather was very hot, and as always when the weather was hot, the praça was teeming with people. He found a place on one of the benches and sat down waiting for Marisa. As he sat, he occasionally glanced towards the clock at the far end of the praça, and at times his eyes followed the gaudily-coloured buses as they snaked their way among the vehicles around the praça.

He had never seen so many buses in his life. There were buses everywhere, each one with different colours, indicating a different line. Also each one carried in front the name of the district in which it was based. He tried now to pronounce the names, which to him sounded like poetry: Maria da Graça, Agua Santa, Bananal, Jardim de Allah, Gardenia Azul – he could go on forever. He was watching the buses, but now he was growing nervous as the hands of the clock climbed to nine.

There were still ten minutes to go. Nevertheless he began keeping his eyes on the entrance of Mac's school. He was now wondering how he should handle this meeting with Marisa. He had thought of this dozens of times. He did not know how to begin talking with her because he did not really feel that he understood her. She had said she liked him – she had even left home in the rain to take a bus ride with him; and yet she seemed unconcerned as to whether or not he went away forever.

On top of all this she had agreed to see him at nine o'clock tonight. Women were really impossible to understand. Anyway it was obvious that she felt something for him if she agreed to see him again.

At the moment there was not much happening in front of Mac's school except people passing up and down the pavement. Craig's eyes shifted to the people inside the praça and to the people milling round the praça. The praça was brightly lit and the Amerindian totem pole placed there as a Carnival decoration was still there, tingeing the place with its coloured lights.

Craig looked back at the clock again and now it was just a few minutes to nine o'clock. His head was filled with Marisa now and he grew so nervous he had to look around at the traffic again to take her off his mind.

As usual there was a flood of vehicles coming down the Rua Conde de Bonfim from Usina. The traffic became stationary for a moment, held up by red traffic lights. When the lights changed, the flow along the cross-street – the Rua General Roca – stopped, and the stream of traffic down the Rua Conde de Bonfim poured down on the praça like an avalanche. At the same time, the cars in the inside lane around the praça moved up to join the traffic passing on the other side, and the vehicles in the outer lane dispersed, giving way to another stream until the traffic lights changed again.

Looking at this was fascinating, although Craig was slightly confused. He could not get accustomed to drivers keeping on the right here and not on the left as in Trinidad. He was not thinking of this deeply, and now he looked back at the clock – and right away his heart began to thump. It was almost nine o'clock now. He got up.

He walked towards the pavement on the Rua Conde de Bonfim side of the praça, keeping his eyes on the entrance of Mac's school. A great number of people were walking by on that pavement and he was anxious not to get confused between passersby and students leaving the school. But he did not intend to cross the road because he wanted to make sure that Mac did not see him tonight.

He stood up just in front of the fountain on the pave-ment side. He was looking at the stairway to Mac's school. His heart was racing. The people who were milling round and round the praça were passing just in front of him now but he did not think of them. There was a stream of vehicles passing and he knew that it was possible that she could slip by unseen and he only hoped that she kept her promise to meet him in the praça tonight.

He was continually being distracted by the people into whose paths he kept finding himself and it was not easy to keep his eyes on Mac's stairway. He began to grow anxious. He could not see the clock from where he was standing, but he reckoned it was already a few minutes past nine and now he was thinking of crossing and going over to Mac's school.

Just as he was waiting to cross at the Rua General Roca he spotted somebody that looked like Marisa walking up to the junction on the other side, but he immediately lost her again in the crowd. Then he saw her again on the far pavement, ready to cross over. He moved back towards the praça side of the pavement and waited for her.

When Marisa arrived on the praça side of the pavement Craig was right there in front of her. On seeing him she cried: 'Oh!'

'You jumping for me, girl? It's me.' He tried to take her hand but at that moment she pretended to fumble with her books, and he left it.

He said: 'How's things – you all right?'

Fine. *Tudo bem.* You made me a fright.'

'So you wasn't even expecting me?'

'I was thinking you would be in the square. How are you?'

'Tudo bem.'

Marisa laughed. 'Oh you are speaking now the Portuguese?'

'I have to try, girl.'

'But your answer is good. So you know *"tudo bem"?'*

'But everybody knows it means "all's well". That's not hard. That's about all the Portuguese I know.'

'Don't worry, when you come back to the Brazil you will soon learn fluent the Portuguese.'

'Yes.' He was surprised to hear her talk about when he came back to Brazil. He was silently glad. He did not say anything.

They walked into the centre of the praça. Although the praça was teeming with people there were still spare seats on the benches and Craig looked around until he found space for two, and they sat down. On one side of them there were lovers embracing. seemingly oblivious of everything. Craig and Marisa paid no attention to them. Craig was still quietly excited over what Marisa had said, and he asked her now: 'How you reached home after that long trip?'

'Very well,' she said. *'You* reached home well?'

'Yes, thanks.' He was looking at her face. It was easy and relaxed. He thought, 'You are a cool customer.'

She said: 'On Saturday you were very tired?'

'Very. Oh God, girl.'

She laughed. 'I told you.'

He said: 'I was very tired and still I couldn't sleep.'

'Why?'

'It's this going back business. I'm so sorry to leave you that I don't want to go again!'

She looked at him wide-eyed. Then she said, light-heartedly: 'Well, don't go.'

'But I have to.'

'I never thought you was in love so much with the Rio.'

'I'm in love with you.'

He turned around to her to see her reaction. She was calm, and smiling. She said: 'Yes, but tell me. You see me only twice, three times, and you say you are in love with me? I don't believe. I don't believe in first sight in love. You see, you are very young. In the Brazil, when a girl is twenty-one like me, she is very serious. When she is in love she will want to marry, and to spend her whole life with that man. You understand? It is not a little thing. Perhaps you can like a person, anybody, but to talk about love, no.'

'So you don't believe what I told you on the bus last Saturday?'

'Yes, I believe you like me.'

'I more than like you, Marisa. True. Believe me.'

'But why?'

'Because – well, I don't know. You are the loveliest black girl in Brazil.'

She laughed. 'And you see already all the black girls in Brazil?'

Craig was noticing that the couple beside them were sitting up now and looking at them. He knew that it was because of the English. He said to Marisa: 'They listening to us.'

She glanced sideways and she saw the two figures paying attention. She said: 'I hope that they do not speak the English.'

'I'm sure they can't.'

She whispered: 'All right, but don't speak too much. There are many people in the Brazil who understand some English.'

'Perhaps a word here and there, but not enough. Anyway, you never know. But you know, Marisa, *you* are a master. I mean, your English is great. It's a good thing you so fluent because otherwise you couldn't know how I feel.'

Marisa did not answer. She thought it would have been a good thing if she didn't know how he felt. She sensed that he was allowing himself to get more and more involved in what he called love and she was careful not to say anything to encourage him.

The crowd was still milling around the praça and the place seemed even more crowded now. There were many more courting couples about and there were sitll some children around the swings. Looking towards Mac's school she suddenly remembered something. She said: 'You know what Mac said today? He said there is a Trinidad office – comércio – here in the Rio. In Flamengo. One of the students say that.'

'Really? You know the address?'

'No, but Mac said he will find out.'

'Well tell Mac that – anyway, don't bother. I'll go to see Mac meself. In fact I was coming to see Mac today, you know, but I couldn't find the time.'

'But you find the time to come to see me.' She turned a quiet smile at him.

He said: 'Naturally. I prefer you to Mac.' And he giggled He added: 'But I must go to see Mac to find out where this place is.'

'It must be in the *catalógo* – how you say – in the telephone directory. Tomorrow I find out for you.'

'That will be fine. Tomorrow I'll come to the school to see Mac and perhaps you'll tell me.'

'Tomorrow I see.'

'Tell Mac to look out for me, I'm coming to see him.'

'All right.'

After a while she said: 'Well, it is nice to talk with you, but I must go now.'

'So suddenly?' He was disappointed.

'I am tired and it is late.'

'All right then. What do you do in the day?'

'I do much work in the house. I am busy. I have no time at all.'

This dashed his hopes. He knew that she was trying to forestall him and this made him feel once again that he had no chance. But he tried to calm himself and he told himself that he must take things easy. Although he was feeling disheartened, he tried to sound cheerful.

'Okay then. Well, I'll come to see Mac tomorrow – and I'll see you.'

'Yes.' She got up. 'Goodbye. *Ciao!*'

'*Ciao!*'

13

Just after half past five the next evening Craig turned up at Mac's school. Mac and Linda were getting ready for the evening's classes. When Mac spotted Craig coming through the door he cried out: 'What happening there, boy. Long time no see.'

'I was to come up before but you know how it is.'

'Yes, I know how it is,' Mac said meaningfully. 'Rio is that sort of place, boy.'

Craig stepped into the office and sat down near the reception desk. Linda was at the reception desk and Mac told her something in Portuguese and she laughed. Craig laughed too, although he did not know what they were talking about. He said: 'You people, eh! By the way how's Linda doing in her English – good?'

'Good! She's next to useless.'

A few students began to trickle in and Craig said: 'Look, I won't hold you up. I only came to find out about some Trade Office Marisa told me about.'

'Oh, yes. One of the students talked about it but let me find out for sure. But don't worry because as soon as I know I'll take you down there.'

'Okay. Right. But you'll find out.'

'Sure. It might be a good place for me to know, too.'

Craig had been thinking of Marisa all the time and now he said in a casual way: 'Marisa here?'

'Marisa? I ain't see her yet. I hear you two going strong.'

'She tell you anything?'

'No. I only know she does see you often.'

Craig looked round. 'You sure that Linda isn't understanding?'

'Not a single thing.'

Craig looked at Linda. She looked up only because she heard her name, but her face was a complete blank. Craig said to Mac: 'Boy, that Marisa girl is tough.'

'Oh, you finding out? You learning fast?'

'And what makes matters worse, she's so damn friendly that you can't tell—'

'Marisa is a very funny girl, boy. Sometimes you think you in something but you ain't in anything. You have to watch that. You see, what you have to watch is this: she naturally likes fellers who talk English. I mean, she'll go out with you just to talk, if you see what I mean.'

'I realise that.'

'I only warning you. It could well be that she like you. Genuine. But I think this is something you have to watch. But I could tell you she's a tough, tough nut to crack, because I know lots of fellers try. She ain't easy, but at the same time she's a hell of a nice girl.'

'She ain't tell you anything about me?'

'No. Not one thing.'

Lots of students were lingering around the reception room now, trying to understand the conversation. Mac was actually talking in a low voice so that they wouldn't understand. Craig realised that it was time for classes and that he was holding matters up. He said now: 'Okay, well I think I'd better run. I'll see you soon, eh? We'll catch up.'

Mac got up. 'Okay, boy. See you. *Ciao*.'

14

Mac found out about the trade office and when he saw Craig again the following week he promised to take him to it. The office was in Flamengo, in the Praia das Americas, and Mac intended to make the journey a sort of excursion, taking along Linda and Marisa, too.

On the Friday morning the four of them caught a bus for Flamengo, from the bus stop in front of the Olinda Cinema. Mac was his usual self, bright and cheerful, and on the bus his English made everyone look round.

He took no notice. The four were sitting in the front portion of the bus. Mac was sitting beside Linda, and just in front of them were Craig and Marisa.

Craig did not speak much for not wanting to attract attention, and Linda was, as always, reserved but Marisa, on the contrary, seemed in a happy mood today, and as they went along she and Mac kept up a lively chatter.

After a while Marisa noticed that no word was coming from Craig, who was beside her, and now she said to him: 'You noticed anything in the square today?'

'Which square?'

'Saens Pena.'

'No.'

'You did not notice the totem pole is not there?'

'Oh, they took the totem pole away?'

Mac said: 'You didn't notice that, boy? Half your life gone.'

Both Mac and Marisa laughed, but Craig only smiled.

Mac and Marisa started a conversation about the totem pole. Marisa wanted to switch to Portuguese for Linda's benefit, but since it would have turned out to be for the benefit of everybody else around them, she kept on talking English. Craig listened to them and was wondering what was really going on between Mac and Marisa. He sat back, thoughtful, looking in front of him, until the bus emerged from a maze of streets and came out into flat, open country. Now there was a glimpse of blue sea in front.

Marisa tapped him on the shoulder: 'All here begins the Flamengo.'

'Oh, I see.'

'Do you know that road there – that we are going to now?'

'No.'

Marisa smiled.

Mac said: 'Boy, you don't know that road?'

'Not really.'

Marisa said: 'That is the *aterro*.'

Craig was genuinely surprised. 'The *aterro*.'

Mac laughed. 'So you see you don't know your Rio yet, boy.'

Craig smiled.

They travelled in silence for a while, with the bus speeding along the *aterro* and then into the Praia do Flamengo. Now Mac began looking out for the place they were going to. He said to Marisa: 'It's somewhere here, eh. I think it's round that corner in front. Keep your hand near the bell-cord.'

'All right.'

Mac stood up, peering through the windows. After a while he said: 'Pull.'

Marisa pulled the bell-cord and the bus stopped.

15

From there, the Trinidad Trade Office was not far away. It was across a little park-like walk, and on the other side of the street called the Praia das Americas. When they got to the office on the second floor of the building, and rang the doorbell, the door swung open and there was the receptionist. The receptionist could not speak English, and as Marisa and Mac began speaking to her in Portuguese a young man hastened to the door.

'Come right in,' he said.

Mac and Craig immediately recognised the accent. As they walked in, the young man showed them to chairs in the hallway, used as a reception room. Mac said: 'Trinidadian, eh?'

'Sure. And I could tell you all from Trinidad, too.'

'Only he and me. The girls are Brazilians.'

'Oh, yes. It's nice to see you all. It's nice to see Trinidadians here.'

'And you are?' Said Mac.

'I'm Alvin, the trade clerk.' He shook hands all round.

By way of introduction, Mac said: 'This girl here is my wife – she is Linda; and this is a friend, Marisa; and he is Craig and I'm Mac.'

'I see. And you fellers living here now?'

'No, no. Craig's only here for a short time. In fact, he's going back next month. But I'm like a native here. I'm here seven years now.'

'Oh, well, you are a real *Carioca*. You even speak the language—'

Craig said: 'Fluent.'

Alvin said: 'And you – how you liking Rio?'

'I like it here a lot. It's a nice place.'

'Rio is nice,' Alvin said.

Mac's eyes were all over the place. After a while he said: 'This office here long?'

'Only about a year now.'

'As long as a year? And we just got to hear about this place! Anyway, you all settling down okay? How you find the language.'

'Well, I don't know. I think I'm getting on all right.'

Marisa was following the conversation and she was thinking what a pleasant, well-groomed person this trade clerk was. His hair was neatly cut, and he was wearing a white shirt with cuff-links, a long, narrow tie with blue polka dots, and his trousers, dark brown, had seams that looked as sharp as razors. His eyes caught her looking at him. He said to Mac: 'And what about these two ladies – I suppose your wife speaks a little English?'

'Nothing at all. But this other one, Marisa, could talk English like a native. She even teaches English.'

'Oh, yes?'

Marisa looked at him with his raised eyebrows and she smiled. He said: 'So your English is fluent, eh?'

'It is not very good.'

'What! Sounds major to me. Where did you take your training and so on?'

'You mean where I learnt? I learnt when I was very small. My father, he was in United States.'

Alvin was thinking to himself: 'Boy, she's tremendous.' She was speaking to him, sitting there elegantly, her legs crossed. He said: 'But your father is not American – he's from over there?'

'No. He was just – what you call it – working. He was working there.'

'I see.' He turned to Mac now. 'Boy, you see how good it is when you learn a language from small? I struggling to learn me Portuguese and this young lady speaking English so comfortable.'

Mac said: 'She bound to be comfortable. She was born in America, you know. And although she came here when she was very young, the old man insisted that they keep up the English. Even he himself learned English.'

'That's great,' Alvin said. 'And the wife doesn't speak any at all?'

'No – Linda doesn't seem to me to be serious. She has opportunities, but up to now she ain't any good at all.'

Alvin said: 'Give her a little more time.' He glanced towards

Linda, who was staring blankly at them. He said: 'You all come and have a look at the place. I can't introduce you to the Chief because he isn't here.'

Mac said: 'It's all right. We only come to see where the place is. We'll come back soon again, man.'

'Okay, but Craig won't be coming back.'

'That's true. Well let's have a quick look.'

Along a corridor they came to a hall, with more offices. In one of them was a middle-aged lady and a young girl.

Alvin said to Craig: 'Come and meet these good people. Dona Ana is the Private Secretary. Vera is a sort of general clerk.'

Craig shook their hands and Dona Ana, smiling shyly, said only. 'Much pleasure.' Mac smiled. Vera reminded him of Linda a little, but that was not the reason why he was pensive.

'Well, this is all the staff we have.'

'But you have a nice little place here – I mean a nice big place,' Craig said.

Mac said politely: 'Yes, this is a very pleasant office.'

Alvin showed them other parts of the office. As he took them round he continued to steal glances at Marisa and secretly he hoped Craig would not come back to this place. He summed up the situation and he said to himself: 'Craig, boy, you look like a nice feller. But it's a good thing you going. Because this is the only thing I want from you.'

16

A few weeks afterwards Mac and Marisa went up to Alto da Boa Vista to bid Craig farewell.

It was the first time the uncle was seeing them, and although he was depressed about Craig having to go, he was very touched that these two should come. The four were all chatting together and in a moment when the uncle saw Craig and Marisa taken up in conversation he tried to draw Mac aside.

He said to him: 'Now about this boy. This thing about him coming back here. What you think?'

Mac looked around him, and he did not want to talk yet.

The uncle said: 'Come out here,' and made a sign with his hand. They had been sitting at the living-room table and now he eased out into the verandah. Mac followed him.

When they got out there the uncle said: 'What is your real opinion? He's my nephew but I don't want him to come back here just for so. The boy may have a big future in Trinidad.'

Mac thought and scratched his head before he replied. He looked down the Rua Ferreira de Almeida and his eyes turned right, towards the mountain. It was approaching dusk and the peak cast stark shadows on the street. Mac turned to the uncle: 'This is a hell of a question. To be frank, I'm for him coming back. This is a big country, and compared to home you have all sorts of opportunities. Personally, I feel he'll be all right here.'

The uncle looked outside and did not say anything at first. He stood staring into space. Then he looked back, towards the door. He said in a very low voice: 'It's not so much the coming back, but the coming back for a woman. First time I seeing the girl. She look all right, but I don't know.'

'Marisa is great.'

'Perhaps, but women, eh?' The uncle shook his head and smiled a bitter smile. He said, 'You know why I here now? I don't know if Craig tell you – perhaps you ain't even business with that, but the thing is, I don't like this thing at all.'

Mac did not say anything. He studied the lank body leaning against the bannister, the head of grey hairs turned away. He imagined he could see Craig in this man.

The uncle turned to Mac almost suddenly, and continued: 'Mister, I does think about this a hell of a lot. I hearing about you all the time so I say I'll talk to you. I frighten for Craig, but what he'll do, he must have a girl. Anywhere he go he must have a girl. But women so treacherous. Now, Craig is my nephew. Suppose when he come back here she with somebody else, what'll he do?'

'Well, get somebody else,' Mac said calmly. Then he laughed. Then growing serious right away he said, 'Uncle, the point is – so far as I know – he ain't coming back here just for a woman. The boy coming back here to live. And let's face it – this is a damn nice place. I hate the Government like hell, but I find the people nice, to tell you the honest truth I find this is a great country to live in. Now me – I'll tell you a little about me because perhaps Craig ain't tell you. I only care about the black man. That's me. And funny, this country is a hell of a country. The system here is against the black man, but the black man could break the system easy, if he use his head. The system is subtle, but we could break it.' He looked at the uncle and smiled. He continued: 'Here the black man have a future. But he must recognise the enemy. He must know what he's fighting for. This is the reason I going to stay here. I here seven years and I staying right here. Brazil is funny. Here ain't have no open pressure, so everybody feel it's all right. And in a way it's all right, because once you know, it ain't so easy again. I mean you get worried like hell. But the pressure here ain't open.'

The uncle said: 'Trinidad ain't have no pressure either.'

Mac exclaimed: 'What?' He was going to explain but he soon thought it a waste of time. He said to himself: 'This man belong to the other generation. If he could spend his whole life in Trinidad and still say that, I'll never convince him.' All he said aloud was, 'Uncle, in Brazil you have to understand the situation. In a subtle way everything is against us. We'll have to overthrow the whole system.'

He was speaking more to himself for he had already assessed the uncle as not being the sort of person who would understand. He said again: 'The whole whole hog would have to go.'

The uncle at once became very fearful. He said, 'Boy, you from Trinidad – you ain't have nothing to do with the Government here.'

Mac smiled and shook his head.

The uncle felt very disappointed and he was certain now that Craig should not come back to get involved in this sort of thing. He said, 'Boy, I frighten for you, yes. You see how the police here does go about with gun and thing? They could shoot you dead just like that.'

Mac looked at him calmly. 'I know.' And to change the conversation, he said, 'But we talking about Craig now.'

The uncle did not say anything.

Mac said, 'This boy could have the world of chances here.'

'But you was just saying how this country was so vicious.'

'Yes, but you can't change it by running away. It's people like Craig we want here. Black fellers with brains. Boys who could make you feel proud.' He put his hand on his companion's shoulder. 'Take it from me, Craig will make good here. This is a big country, with a lot of opportunities, and in a way you don't get the kind of pressure you get in Trinidad. Here they can't keep down a boy with education. This country too big for that.'

The uncle again found himself being swayed. He said, 'But what about a job? Where he'll work? He can't even talk the damn language.'

'The language ain't nothing. You think he is you?' Mac laughed. He said, 'The boy is keen and he'll learn fast. But from the first he'll have to mark time at my school. Teaching. But he'll move up so fast you yourself will be surprised.'

The uncle remained silent for a while, thinking, then he said, 'This is a hell of a big step to take.'

Mac said, 'Everybody have to take a big step some time or other. Look, I came here seven years ago, and that was a big step too. But I took it.'

'Why you came here? – if I could ask—?'

'I came here because everybody used to tell me that in Brazil every man is a man.'

'But it ain't.'

'I know it ain't.'

'The poor man is still a dog, like at home.'

'Well, that part of it, you'll never be able to change that. The

poor man is a dog all over the world. But what does really rile me—
' He stopped talking as the verandah door opened.

Marisa came out into the verandah followed by Craig. She
seemed as calm as always, but Craig looked disturbed.

The uncle said, 'We out here, just exchanging ideas.'

Craig said, 'We, too. We was exchanging ideas too.'

The uncle looked at them and he sensed that something was
amiss. Outwardly he tried to appear bright. He said: 'By the by,
nobody ain't take a drink yet? What the france is this! Come let's
have a drink, man. I forget that completely.'

They all followed him inside.

After the uncle had filled glasses all around, Mac continued,
'So as I was saying, I came then and it wasn't exactly what I heard –
that's putting it mildly – but I liked the country somehow, and I stayed.
I was up in Bahia and I married a Brazilian girl – to be a Brazilian
quick, you know – and I moved down here.'

The uncle was amazed. He said, 'So you take up this Brazilian
business right away? And how you fighting up with the language?'

'Well I learned Portuguese in a jiffy. I mean, the wife is Brazilian.'

'Oh, so you talk it good?'

'Fairly,' Mac said.

Marisa said, 'It is not "fairly". Mac, he is very good at
Portuguese. He is much better than I speak English.'

The uncle said, 'This is my only trouble. This language. I can't
get to like Portuguese. If I could get to like Portuguese I'll speak it,
but I can't get to like it.'

Mac said, 'So you can't talk the lingo at all?'

'No. I'll never talk this.'

Marisa smiled. Mac said, 'How long you here, Uncle?'

'Five years.'

'And you make out five years without speaking Portuguese?'

'Whole five years. I mean I could say a word or two but I can't
talk anything fluent.'

'And you get on all right?'

'All right? Ha, boy.' The uncle shook his head.

Mac looked at the dejected face. He rested his drink on the
table. He knew that the uncle had quite a lot of things inside him, but
this was not the time and place to set him talking. He just said,

'Sometimes a language can't come at all, then all of a sudden you have it. You ever experienced that?'

'No.'

'Well that does happen.'

The two men continued talking and Marisa watched them and whispered to Craig. 'Your family cannot get him to come back? He is torture with homesick.'

Craig was still sullen but he smiled a little. 'Uncle is not homesick, but he has a lot of worries and sometimes he gets depressed. It's a funny thing, but on the whole he doesn't mind Brazil. He likes Brazil.'

'It is a funny thing to like Brazil?' Marisa looked at him questioningly.

'I never said that.'

Their voices were low. Now there was silence for a while and there was silence on his uncle's side too. He looked at his uncle. The uncle's eyes were blank, and as often was the case, his mind was in Port of Spain. He was truly homesick, and he was thinking of the woman who had make him run away. And he was thinking of the man who had taken his place. He did not want to be among them – he did not want to be anywhere near them – but he was always thinking of them. He was thinking now of his married life, which had been a disaster, and he felt that no woman – none whatsoever – was to be trusted.

Mac, seeing the old man silent and depressed, got up and went into the verandah. Marisa wanted to go and join Mac in the verandah but she thought she'd remain because of Craig. He was behaving so unpredictably tonight.

There was complete silence round the table. After a while Mac came back and sat down. He said, 'Nobody ain't talking? Uncle, I like the little surroundings.'

'Oh, you like up here? It's nice. It's a little cold, though.'

Mac said: 'Yes, because it's right up on the mountain. Uncle, you was nearly on the peak?' There was laughter. Marisa looked at Craig and saw that even *he* chuckled.

The uncle said: 'Nearly on the peak is right. I like here. But I didn't choose it, I—' He was going to explain, then he stopped, and he said with sudden cheerfulness, 'Look, I make a little cook-up, you know. A *pelau*.'

Mac said: 'Oh God, and you holding it back so long? You know how long I ain't eat *pelau?*'

The uncle laughed.

Marisa asked Craig, 'What is *pelau?*'

Mac's voice was above theirs: 'You know how long I ain't had this thing? Since Trinidad. That is my favourite, Unc. Good thing I come up here.'

The uncle was smiling and he was feeling very happy that Mac was excited about the *pelau*. He got up to go to the kitchen and Marisa went with him to help. Mac and Craig remained. Mac had of course realised that something was amiss between Craig and Marisa, and so he wanted to strike up a conversation with Craig but without mentioning the girl.

He looked at the bottle of *cashasa* on the table. He had brought it but they had not opened it yet. He said to Craig: 'You ever drink that?'

'No. Not really. What drink is that.'

'It's rum. But like raw rum. Like that drink in Trinidad we call mountain dew. You can't take much, but it's good.'

'I must try it.'

'Don't try it now, though. We could take something after we eat. That on an empty stomach, boy, could send you pitching. After we eat we'll break the seal.'

'Okay, I'll really like to have a taste.'

'They make this here a lot. And sell it in shops, you know. Not like mountain dew. Look Uncle bringing the *pelau*.'

The uncle's *pelau* was an attempt at the Brazilian dish, *feijoada*, and in it there was a lot of salted meat, and rice, and a lot of ochroes and melongene, and other vegetables that he had grown around the house. They all liked it – especially Marisa, who had not had it before. Mac, too, was greatly enjoying it, but from time to time he praised it profusely just to make the Uncle feel good.

The uncle himself ate little. Most of the time he was deep in thought. He was thinking about the three young people and he was somewhat disturbed. He noticed his nephew's sullenness and he felt there was more in this than the fact that the boy was leaving for Trinidad. He wondered if it was jealousy. In fact he noticed the warm feeling that existed between Mac and Marisa and this made him ponder even more. Because from appearances it really looked as if it was Mac she was attached to.

He watched them eating and said nothing. He liked Marisa, who, although she had come here for the first time, seemed so comfortable and at home. He listened to her English, and although it was good, it was quaint, and sometimes it sounded 'wrong-sided'. This brought a faint smile to his face.

Every few moments he thought of his nephew sitting silently on the other side of the table. It was obvious that something was wrong. The uncle wondered if in fact there *was* something to be jealous of. He did not know what part Mac was playing – in fact he did not know Mac at all, he felt. But his impression was that this was an open and honest man. But he could not decide. Things were certainly strange. Judging Mac and Marisa on the surface, he liked them both, but Craig's manner made him feel upset, and, at times, deeply suspicious. In his own case he had taken years to find out what his own wife had been doing. Women could be cruel.

The uncle only half-heard the talking going on between Marisa and Mac. Now he was thinking of his own situation – his having settled down in this country that he could never grow to love, that he could never think of as home. He was thinking of how he had trusted so completely, and how he was now marked for life, inside.

He did not want Craig to face this sort of thing, but if he was stubborn he would face it. Because to him, Marisa was not really in love. At least, not with Craig. In any case, something had gone wrong tonight. He did not see any point in his nephew coming back.

Mac interrupted his thoughts: 'Oh God, Uncle, that was a nice *pelau*.'

'Oh, you finish. You want more?'

'No, I can't eat no more.' Mac rested his hands on his belly.

The uncle laughed. He looked at Marisa: 'More?'

'More, no. But I enjoyed it.'

'Thank you.'

Mac said, 'No, it's thanks to *you*.'

Craig was finished eating too, but he did not say anything.

After a few moments Mac said to him, 'You want to hit the *cashasa* now?'

There was a strained smile: 'Not right now.'

'Try some *cashasa*, Mar.'

'Me, no. Only I will take some wine.'

'Okay, you have wine. Uncle will take a drink with me.'

The uncle said, 'Look, boy, I don't know. I doesn't drink at all, you know. And I hear about this thing, *cashasa* – look, when I ready I'll have a little sip.'

Mac said, 'But what is this! I buy this drink for me alone then! Okay, we'll christen it.'

He broke the seal.

17

The Uncle was persuaded to try the *cashasa* and after a few drinks he got up and went and sat down in an easy chair and it was not long before he felt overcome with sleep. He sipped a glass of the *cashasa* and he was thinking far. Craig had been drinking some wine but now he felt like trying out the *cashasa* and he poured some into his glass.

Mac was watching. 'Not so much. Take it easy, boy. This Brazilian rum don't make joke.'

Craig smelled it and then he tasted it. He savoured it on his tongue a bit, feeling amidst the burning, the tang of cane juice. Then he swallowed it down and felt his mouth on fire. He said, 'It's nice.'

Mac said, 'Watch that drink. It would get you tipsy in two two's.'

'This is good cane juice, boy.'

Mac laughed.

'Why they call it *cashasa*?'

'I don't know.'

Craig poured more drink into his glass. The uncle was already dozing off in the chair and Craig looked back at him and said in a low voice: 'The old boy nodding off. You know how sorry I does feel for him? My heart really hurting me to go back and leave him.'

Mac felt that perhaps it was Marisa Craig's heart was hurting him to leave, but he did not say anything. He looked back at the uncle's head, which was occasionally butting the air. The uncle, although past middle age, was still rather young-looking. His age showed only through the lines that were beginning to appear on his cheeks, and through the white hairs on the sides of his head.

Craig said to Mac: 'This man had more horns than ten cows.'

They laughed. Mac said. 'You know, in my experience – believe you me – it's only the good men that does get that kind of people. I imagined it was something like that.'

Craig had his eyes on the kitchen but now he turned to Mac

again. 'Even since I was a little feller going to school, my uncle seeing hell. And as you see he is really a good, simple man. I does feel so sorry for him.'

Mac nodded his head.

Craig continued, This lady – I don't call her no *aunt* – this so-and-so had a lot more brains than he, and she made him hop. And she was good-looking? Big, dreamy eyes, boy. She was two-timing him from the start, and he didn't know a thing. She is – let me see – ten, fifteen years younger than he, so you could imagine the woman still looking young. Boy, this man see hell.' He shook his head. 'And this is my favourite uncle, you know. Christ, when I think of this I does get so vex. He shoulda kill that blasted woman.'

'Don't talk about kill.'

'I say he shoulda kill the bitch.'

Craig had suddenly raised his voice and Mac looked now to see whether it had roused the old man. The uncle was lying back on the easy chair, snoring, his head canted sideways, his mouth open.

Mac turned back to Craig and forced a smile. He noticed that Craig's eyes were slightly red now. There was not much *cashasa* in Craig's glass and what was at the back of Mac's mind now was to try and get the bottle away from him. He wanted to do so without Craig noticing and he did not quite know how to do it. As he was thinking about this Marisa came in from the kitchen, and Craig's head, which had begun to hang, jerked up. Marisa was amused to see the uncle sleeping so comically in the chair and she stood up and looked at him. Now she sat down on the very seat the uncle had left round the table, and she said, '*Cashasa* makes that, no?'

Craig said, 'He ain't even touch his *cashasa*.' As he spoke, his breath reeked with the liquor.

Marisa said to Mac, 'And what subject for you two.'

'We just talking in general. Nothing special.'

Craig turned round to her and said, 'We talking about how woman bad.' And he laughed.

There was silence. Mac looked at Craig. Craig seemed to be tense, in spite of the laughter. Marisa was, as usual, calm. After a few moments she said, 'So Craig, you will be in the air in a little time?'

'Yes, but I ain't get a chance to talk to you yet.'

Mac said, 'That is true. I mean that is really facts, Marisa. After all, the man going tomorrow and you all ain't talking your business at all? If he has to come back, now is the time to talk about this and plan. The best thing for me to do – don't feel bad – the best thing is for me to go home and leave you two alone. So Craig—'

'Mac, do not go, please.' Marisa suddenly became frantic as she saw Mac get up.

Craig flashed a glance at her. He said to Mac, 'Oh, you two discuss it already?'

'Discuss what? Why? Marisa is her own woman, she ain't have to discuss nothing with me.'

Craig was angry, and at the same time he was consumed with jealousy and frustration. He blurted out, 'Look Mac, I don't know if Marisa want me or who she want. We have a plan that I'll come back here for her, but she getting on so funny tonight I don't know what she intend to do. And yet if I come back here *she* is the reason.'

Marisa said, 'Me? I am a reason?' Craig had been talking so fast she understood little of what he said.

Craig said, 'But you agreed for me to come back.'

'Me?' Marisa was growing distressed. Mac began to breathe heavily. He said, 'Well let's put it this way: you engaged to her?'

Craig did not answer. Mac went on, 'I'm not interfering, but let's look at it. You flying out of this place tomorrow. You want to come back but you don't know when you'll make it. You think a girl will decide to just sit down like that and wait for you? I mean if you two was engaged it's a different story.'

Craig said, 'You know damn well we ain't engaged.'

This was so sudden and sharp that there was no sound for a moment. Then Mac said, 'Okay, I finish. This problem is not my problem. It's time for me to go.'

Marisa got up from the chair. 'I go too.'

Craig raised his voice, 'Mac, I'll be frank. As a man I'll be frank with you. If you want Marisa you could take Marisa, Right?'

Both Mac and Marisa looked at him flabbergasted. Then Mac shook his head and smiled. Then he walked towards the uncle who was snoring in the chair. He put his hands on the uncle's shoulders as though he were going to shake him, but before he did so he turned round to Craig.

'You ain't the only one,' he said. 'All sorts of people does think I and Marisa in something. I and Marisa ain't in nothing. Take it easy. The honest truth is, with this school I have here, I was glad for you and Marisa to get together because I will gain a hell of a lot.'

Craig said, 'If I don't come back you'll gain a hell of a lot.'

'Please,' Marisa said, 'Please do not speak like that.'

Mac said, 'Leave him. Leave him. You don't know that *cashasa* does make people talk their mind?'

Marisa was trembling, leaning up against the table. Mac wanted to hold her but he refrained. Marisa continued talking, and it was in Portuguese now. Mac said, 'Mar, try to talk English. Take your cool time and talk English. Let him know what you saying.'

Marisa said, 'I am saying that I did not promise the Craig anything. On the bus I told him I said if you want to come back to the Brazil you can come back but I cannot say that you must come back for me.'

Craig almost shouted, 'And that is all you said?'

Mac said to him, 'Not so loud. You'll wake up the old man.'

'If he wake up he wake up!'

Marisa herself wanted the uncle to wake up because she was growing afraid. She knew that Craig was under the influence of the *cashasa* and she did not know how the argument would end. Now she walked around Mac and she shook the uncle.

The uncle opened his eyes and tried to nod out the sleep from his head. Marisa took up her handbag from the table.

Craig said, 'Where you going!' and he got up.

The uncle said, 'What's that. What – what happening here!'

Mac was suddenly breathing fast. He felt the blood rush up to his head and he stood there staring at Craig. Trying to be calm, he said, 'Boy, if the girl don't want you, you'll make a noise for that? Watch what you doing, boy. You like trouble?' Then Mac turned to Marisa. 'Let's go.'

As Marisa moved off Craig jerked her back by the hand and then as she saw Mac rushing towards him he let her go and swung towards the table to pick up a bottle. Mac rushed and held his hand before he could reach the bottle. The uncle cried, 'Oh God!' and hurried to separate them, but the easy chair lay between and he had to go around the table. Marisa was pulling Mac back from behind but as Mac's hold on Craig loosened, Craig caught him with a punch on the jaw and Mac fell back. Now as Craig rushed forward Marisa managed to get between him and Mac and in that interval some heavy blows from Craig landed on her head.

She cried out, 'You *malandro filho da puta, porcaria*'

Mac was now like a tiger enraged. Now with his back against the front door he had Craig folding in two with a kick against the belly, and as Craig went back, Mac screamed to Marisa, 'Pass! Get out of this blasted room.' Craig caught himself momently and rushed back, and the uncle held him, but he wrenched himself away and with the same action he grabbed a glass and shied it at Mac's head, Mac ducked and it shattered the pane of the front door.

The uncle cried, 'Oh God, all you stop!'

Craig lunged for another glass but Mac took up a chair and thrust it at him then he held on to one end of the table and tilted it over, sending it crashing with glasses and bottles onto the floor.

Craig screamed, 'Oh God, Uncle, where the cutlass!' And he dashed into the kitchen.

At the mention of cutlass Mac disappeared through the front door. He saw Marisa in the verandah and pulled her with him down the concrete steps and into the road. He cried, 'Come on. Run. Come on, man. Run girl – you, donkey!' She kicked off her shoes and he snatched them up, and they ran pell-mell into the dark.

They did not run right down the Rua Ferreira de Almeida. They turned right into a little cross street, and then they turned left, and then not hearing footsteps behind them, Marisa stopped to put on her shoes. Then they went on again, and now they took a short cut, amongst bushes, to the Floresta da Tijuca. When they came out of Tijuca Forest they got on to a short road which led to a praça where the bus for Praça Saens Pena took up passengers. They sat down on one of the benches, waiting. The night was pitch black. They were panting too much to speak.

18

Just about a week afterwards the trade clerk telephoned the Instituto MacWilliams de Idiomas. He was anxious to get in touch with Marisa again and knowing that Craig was now safely in Trinidad, he telephoned the school.

Mac's wife answered. Alvin said, 'Mr MacWilliams, please.'

'Mr MackyWilliams he not here.'

'Could I leave a message?'

There was silence,

'Could you give him a message for me?'

'I no speak the English.'

Alvin changed to Portuguese and told her that he was the person at the Trade Office whom Mac had visited. Mac's wife did not seem to know about this but she said, 'Mr MackyWilliams when he come he telephone for you.'

'Marisa there?' And he repeated the question in Portuguese.

'No, *senhor*. Six *horas* she here.'

'Okay, I'll telephone again at six o'clock.'

There was silence.

'That's all right with you?'

'No speak it the English.'

'But you speaking English all the time,' Alvin chuckled.

'Yes, *senhor*, Mr MackyWilliams when he come he telepone for you.'

'Okay, *Ciao*!'

'Goodbye.'

Alvin put down the telephone and then walked out into the hall and into the big open recess where the receptionist, Vera, sat. Vera was sticking newspaper cuttings onto sheets of typing paper and putting these sheets into folders. Alvin said, 'Vera, I want—' then he stopped. He had forgotten that she too, spoke no English. He then asked her in Portuguese whether the trade commissioner had slipped in. She said no.

Vera went on with her work and he stood there watching her paste the cuttings onto the sheets of paper. They were all sorts of trade cuttings, mainly from Trinidad and Brazilian newspapers. Mr Wilkes, the Trade Commissioner, always marked thing out for her to cut.

Alvin was looking at her but he was not thinking of her and the clippings. He was thinking of Marisa. He intended to talk to the trade commissioner about her, to try to get her a job there. He had not tackled it yet because he wanted to talk to Marisa herself first. He hoped everything would work out all right. Sometimes Mr Wilkes could be very difficult. Alvin was not even sure that it was wise to have Marisa working with him at the trade office. But the way Mac had talked he was determined to try anyway.

The blinding glare of the late March sun almost hurt his eyes. He bent and looked down at the Praia das Americas beneath him, and as usual it was cluttered with parked vehicles, and there were a few Volkswagen taxis speeding by. He looked beyond the street to the *praça* on the other side where there was a huge statue. Beyond the statue, and the Praia do Flamengo, and the carriageways of the *aterro,* there was a glimpse of blue sea.

He said to himself, 'O God, this Rio is a nice place!'

Vera looked up. Although he was not looking at her now he saw the movement of her head and realised that he had spoken aloud. He looked round and she asked him if he was talking to himself. Speaking Portuguese, he repeated what he said, and they both laughed. She was thrilled.

Whenever he looked out from here he was always fascinated. To him it was always breathtaking to watch how the land swung in with a big curve and curled out again to form this nearby blue bay, the *Enseada da Gloria.* Beyond the *Enseada da Gloria* there was Guanabara Bay, dotted with little islands now glinting in the sun like jewels. The hazy mountains in the distance were the hills of Niteroi.

He glanced at Vera who was now looking at him as if she wanted to say something. She carefully prepared the words on her tongue, and now as he turned round to her, she said, 'You like?'

He said, 'Sure. I like very much.'

She laughed. She was pleased because she had spoken English

and Alvin understood. She carried on sticking down her clippings and dreaming of herself conversing in English.

Alvin himself was day dreaming. Truly, he liked Rio. Now, after two years, he felt himself a part of the country. He had felt homesick, until he learned the language, but sometimes he now forgot that he ever spoke English. It was only when people like Mac and Craig came to the trade office that he became the other Alvin–Alvin the Trinidadian.

The thought of Mac and Craig made his mind slip to Marisa again. He wanted to mention her to Vera, but he decided against it. He did not know how things would turn out. Sometimes girls raised hopes only to get you excited and afterwards they were never the same towards you. He looked once more at the street below, then he pushed himself off from the window and ambled back to his desk.

He had gone to look out to see if Mr Wilkes was coming. He had reached a point where he had to see Mr Wilkes before he could continue. He looked at his watch. It was nearly half-past eleven. He wondered if the chief would show up before lunchtime.

He thought of Marisa and the job. If she was taken on there it would certainly be a great help to her. He did not know how much Mac was paying her but if she was only doing part-time work it was bound, to be next to nothing! It would be really fine if she could get a job at the trade office–whether or not things worked out between them. And afterwards, if she liked, she could continue teaching at Mac's school on evenings. This would be a very good arrangement because in that case he would not be depriving Mac of anything. He was anxious to do something that would please Marisa. He was impatient to speak to her again and relieved that he had something to say to her. He only hoped that Mac's wife did not forget to pass on the message.

Mr Wilkes did not come in before lunch and Alvin was about to step out when the telephone rang. When he took up the telephone the voice said, 'Hi! What's up?' It was Mac at the other end.

'Oh, it's you? What happening?'

'Linda said you rang.'

Alvin lowered his voice. 'Yes. Well–we have a vacancy for a translator. I thought maybe Marisa—'

He stopped. Mac said, 'You think she could get that job?'

'Why not? That should be easy for her. I hope you don't mind.'

'But of course not.'

'She could continue teaching at your school, you know. We only go up to five o'clock.'

Mac had not thought of this. 'Oh yes! That's great. That's fine. You all offering her the job?'

'I ain't talk to the chief yet.'

'I hope it won't be no problem offering her that job.'

'How you mean "problem".'

Mac said, 'Boy, I does talk frankoment too bad. I ain't no diplomat. I does notice things and the trouble with me is I does talk what I notice.'

'What you notice?'

'Well let's put it in a nice way. We on the phone. Marisa looks more like a Trinidadian than your Vera and your so-called bilingual secretary. I mean, she is more one of *us*, if you know what I mean. When it comes to this sort of thing, especially in our own place, I just have to talk.'

There was silence from Alvin's end.

Mac said, 'You get me?'

'I get you.'

This time the silence was long and awkward and to break it Alvin said, 'This boy, Craig. He drop you or Marisa a line yet?'

This question had Mac stuttering. He ended up saying that he did not know if Marisa had got a letter.

Alvin said, 'They still going good, of course.'

'I think so. Boy, I really don't know.'

'When you all coming this way?'

'We'll come anytime. When you talk to your man there. I mean, if you fix up an interview for Marisa, she must come, and I'll make the trip with her. Anyway, I'll ask her to phone you.'

'All right, let her phone. But let her phone after I talk to Wilkes. Let's say Monday.'

'Right.'

'We'll see what happening,' Alvin said. Although he himself had suggested Monday, he felt very depressed to have to wait until then.

19

Alvin did not get the opportunity to talk to Mr Wilkes for the rest of that day, nor the next, and when he came into the office on Monday morning he received such a shock that he telephoned Mac immediately.

When Mac answered the telephone, Alvin said, 'Mac, it look as if Marisa out of luck.'

Why? What happen?'

'There's some girl sitting down in the reception and Vera said it's the new translator.'

'You making joke?'

'No. I'm serious. The Chief didn't tell me a thing. Boy, it have me reeling.'

'What sort of girl it is?'

Alvin did not answer right away.

Mac asked again. 'What sort of person?'

'Well, you know, the usual.'

Mac said, 'Stupes!' Then he said, 'This does hurt me down in my guts.'

'Anyway, you'll tell Marisa what happened.'

'You'd better tell her yourself. When she come in I'll ask her to ring you.'

'Okay.'

Mac said, 'Al, boy, you seeing for yourself how things tough on us?'

'Yes, but you know, our girls–they don't seem to come forward— '

'When you fellers lean backwards on the other side, how they'll come forward?'

'You saying "You fellers". Don't blame me. Tell Wilkes.'

'If I talk to Wilkes I'll cuss him.'

Alvin was silent.

Mac said, 'Anyway, I know I'm odd like hell, I know I'm different from most of our fellers. In Trinidad they used to call me radical. They used to say I'm extreme. Anyway I have to leave you now, boy. I have to rush down to *Centro* now. When I see Marisa this evening I'll tell her to ring you. She'll be here around six.'

'Okay, I'll be right here in this office. I'll wait right here.'

'Okay.'

Alvin went through the day depressed. Mr Wilkes came in at about ten o'clock and soon afterwards he buzzed Vera and she went in to him and returned for the new girl. After a while Mr Wilkes emerged with the new girl and took her into Alvin's office.

After the introduction Mr Wilkes said, 'I'm taking on this young lady as a translator. She is from the Pacheco University. Her father was ambassador here in Rio.'

'Oh, yes?'

'Her English is fluent.'

'Oh.'

'I'll send you her details later.'

'All right, Sir.'

When Mr Wilkes and the young lady went out, Alvin said to himself, 'Oh, she's a big fish!' He thought of Marisa and now he was even more depressed. There was a lot of work to do but now he just sat and stared at the table before him. Then he began to work a little, but without enthusiasm. As the day passed he said very little to Vera and nothing at all to the new girl, whose desk was facing Vera across the recess. He remained gloomy and silent until it was five o'clock and they all left.

After five o'clock he got up and went to the window. Now he was anxious and restless for Marisa's telephone call. He could not do any more work and now he thought of going to his home in Copacabana and coming back before six. But he was scared that Marisa would telephone while he was out. Although he was feeling dejected, he felt great anxiety to be in contact with Marisa again and he was nervous and excited at the prospect of hearing her voice again.

Now he wondered how clearly she remembered him from that last time. He was sure there had been some spark of attraction on her part and he wanted to see if he was right. He hoped to God that he was right. Nevertheless he was bracing himself for disappointment.

He was quite prepared for her saying that she did not remember him at all. Girls were like that. Sometimes they pretended, and sometimes they just did not remember. But the boys remembered every little detail. He remembered Marisa exactly as she was that day she came to the trade office.

The anxiety was overbearing and he thought he would step out a little. He went downstairs, crossed the Praia das Americas, and walked into the little garden-square opposite. Looking at his watch he saw that it had turned half past five. He sat down on one of the benches and looked at the huge statue before him. The statue bore the name 'Almir-ante Barroso'. He did not know what that was.

He got up after a little while and walked around the column. Then he looked up and down the Praia do Flamengo, then towards the *aterro,* then towards the sea, and afterwards he looked at his watch. It was a quarter to six. His heart began to thump. He turned and started to walk back.

When he reached the office it was still ten minutes to six o'clock and he ambled about a little then went to the newspaper and magazine stand to look at the recent Trinidad newspapers. As he started to peruse them he had to rush to the telephone.

He said, 'Hello.'

'Mr Alvin?'

'Hello Marisa, how are you?' A storm of relief broke over him.

'I am well. And how are you?'

'Not bad. I've been so anxious to see you and Mac back here.'

'Mac said he will come?'

'I told Mac you two could come anytime. After all!'

She did not follow the 'after all', but she said, 'We will come.'

'All right. Come soon. Mac gave you a message from me today?'

'He said for me to telephone you.'

'Well what happened is – I was trying to get a job here for you, but things didn't work out. You know.'

'A job for me?'

'They had a translating job going but the chief gave it to somebody else.'

'Oh.'

'You aren't disappointed?'

'I did not know much about this.'

'Mac didn't tell you?'

'I think he told me something like that.'

'Anyway, girl, I'm sorry they took somebody else.'

'It is all right. Don't worry.'

'I must worry. I'd give anything to have you working here.'

His heart raced. He paused to hear what she would say. He thought he heard faint chuckling.

He said, 'You heard me?'

'Yes. *Obrigada* – thank you.' She chuckled again, then she said, 'I have to go back to teach now.'

'When I'll see you?'

'I do not know.'

'Marisa, I wanted to ask you this – I wanted to ask you if you remembered me at all.'

'*Claro*. Sometimes—' And she stopped.

'Sometimes what?' Alvin felt excited. He stood with the telephone pressed to his ears.

'Sometimes I remember you very well.'

He did not question her further. He felt as if he had already won, He said, 'Thank you. I remember you all the time. In fact, I've been thinking of you ever since you all came here'

She said, 'I see. All right. I have to go back to teach now.'

'What about Craig?'

Marisa was embarrassed. She did not know what to reply.

'Eh?' Alvin said. 'What about you and Craig?'

'About me and Craig?' She said. Then she hesitated. She did not know if Mac had told him about that night.

'Alvin said, 'You two going strong? When's he coming back?'

'I do not know.' And then she said, 'Craig and me, we did not end up very well.'

'No? What happened? Why?'

'We did not do very well at the *despidida* – what you call it?'

'*Despidida*. I see, the farewell. Oh, the farewell party didn't go so good?' He wondered if they had quarrelled but he did not want to ask.

Now she said, 'I have to go back to teach. I am late.'

'When I'll see you?'

'I do not know. I am so busy.'

'What about later on in the week?'

'I am too busy later on in the week.'

'What about next week then?'

'Perhaps.'

He tried to appear calm but his voice trembled with excitement. 'What day?'

'I will ask Mac to see what day he can come.'

Alvin said 'stupes' in disgust and there was soft chuckling at the other end. He said, 'But, I mean, you have to ask Mac? You can't come here by yourself?'

'I am coming with Mac. You don't want me to come, no?'

'Yes, please come. I'm depending on that.'

He could hear her soft laughter. She said, 'I will go to see you on Monday with Mac and perhaps on the Friday I go to the Trade Office alone to see you.'

A wave of relief and joy swept over Alvin. He did not want to continue talking much longer now. He did not want to give her any time to change her mind.

He said, 'Okay, then. So I'll see you on Monday then.'

'Monday, yes.'

'Till then, be good.'

'Goodbye. *Ciao!*'

'*Ciao!*'

20

.When Alvin saw them he was excited and glad. He said to Mac: 'Nice to see you again.'

Mac beamed. Alvin was sincerely happy to see Mac, but overwhelmed to see Marisa. He did not say anything to her directly. He said to them, 'You could come right over to my office.'

Marisa was looking neat and elegant and Alvin glanced at her but he did not feel to say anything to her yet. Mac, too, looked very smart. He had on a brown, well-seamed suit and a bright Trinidad tie, and his shoes were shining like mirrors. His hair was well-groomed and parted in the middle, and he was clean-shaven. There were two black wisps of a moustache under his nose.

'Sweetman,' Alvin thought, and laughed to himself. He placed chairs for the two to sit down, Mac said, 'We mustn't keep you long.'

'You have to go out?'

'No, we only came here. I only came along with Marisa, really.'

'You looking so smart.'

'Me?'

'You and Marisa.' He looked towards her and they both smiled.

Mac said, 'No, we wanted to come to find out about this job you talked about. Now, what really happen?'

Mac and Marisa were both seated right up to Alvin's desk and Mac started to look tense.

Alvin said, 'Boy, I don't know how the job went like that.' He turned to Marisa, 'You see that girl sitting outside there – the one in the green dress; that's the one who got it.'

Mac said, 'But why oh why things have to be like that. Why you people couldn't give Marisa the job – or even a girl *like* Marisa.'

Alvin looked at the door. He said in a low voice, 'Wilkes still here, I don't want to go into any long explanation now. We'll talk, and I'll tell you exactly what happened. It's not any funny business.'

'It doesn't look funny to you?'

'Yes, in a way. But—'

'In a way? Boy you making fun. Three of them and not one like you, and you saying it look funny *in a way* ?'

Alvin saw that Mac was getting excited and he was only hoping that Mr Wilkes did not come in. He said to Mac, 'We'll talk.'

He felt very upset about what Mac was seeming to imply and he looked at Marisa to see how she reacted. Marisa looked unruffled. As she saw him look at her she smiled a little. Their eyes fixed each other for a moment.

Mac said, 'Boy, I worried like hell, yes. What will happen to our nice black girls?'

'You mean here in Brazil?' Alvin said.

'I don't only mean here, I mean here, there, and everywhere. I worried like france. Something have to happen. I mean, take for instance you man here – Wilkes – he blind or something? After all, he mustn't forget that in this Trade Office it's Trinidad, you know. And in Trinidad we are people too. We *must* help black Brazilians.'

Alvin did not say anything and Marisa looked at him and found that he seemed confused. She said now, 'Don't worry. Mac, he is always political.'

'So this is political! You see what I mean? Boy, my heart does hurt me down in my guts when I hear these people talk. You'll call what I say "political"?'

Alvin said, 'No. You talking facts;'

'Anyway, you can't tell a black Brazilian nothing about race. Not only Marisa, all of them think the same way. It's distressing. They can't see what's going on around them.'

Marisa still seemed unruffled. She and Alvin were both silent. Mac continued, 'And they bloody well trailing behind everybody else. This is facts, not politics.'

Marisa looked at him and said quite calmly, 'It is facts. I agree. But you do not know the Brazil. Here it is a huge country, and – what you call it – the change have to be slow. You do not understand. The *escravos* – I do not know how to explain.'

Mac said to Alvin, *Escmvos* is slaves. But it's no point she bringing up slavery as an excuse.'

'The Brazil was the last place for slaves,' Marisa said.

'I know, I know,' Mac said. 'I know they abolished slavery here in the 1880s or something. Long after every place else. But that ain't have much to do with it. If you had a Government—'

'It is always the Government, no? The group of your friends, UNE, is always blaming. And you say that you are not political.'

'UNE doesn't come into that. And in any case I'm only a member of UNE, that's all.'

As Marisa was about to reply the Trade Commissioner walked in. He was a tall, military-looking man, very stiffly dressed. As he walked into the room Mac stood up, and then Marisa stood up too. Mr Wilkes smiled with Mac and Marisa. He took some papers from Alvin and he went out of the room.

Mac whispered, 'We okay here? I mean, if we have to go, say, you know.'

'Oh, that's all right.'

Mac sat down again. After a few moments he said, 'Yes, As we were saying. Marisa is always bringing up this UNE. She thinks—'

'What is UNE?'

Marisa said, 'UNE? It is the political students. It is for the letters: Uniaõ Nacional de Estudantes – they want to break up the Brazil.'

Mac shook his head and smiled. He looked at Alvin. 'According to the Government UNE is Communist. Anything that is for the people, you know, is Communist. Look, I don't know much about UNE, eh. All I know is that it is a set of students who want to put things right in Brazil – but of course that is Communism.' He looked at Marisa. She said nothing. But she was not so unruffled now. Mac continued, 'I don't think you know anything about UNE so I'll tell you. It's a bunch of students who is damn fed up with the Government. They say so in the open – not Mac – and a lot of them get clamped in jail, too. The trouble started up over university places. The Government wanted to close down universities right, left and centre, because they say the universities causing trouble, the students asking too many questions,' he laughed. 'What the Government is afraid of is education for everybody. The people will get too wise.'

'*Bobagem,*' Marisa said, 'Nonsense.'

Mac said, 'Look, Alvin, you here for a little while and you ought to know what the position here is like. The poor man here ain't have a chance to get any education.'

Marisa said, 'If you don't like the Brazil why you don't go to live in Trinidad?'

'Take it easy. Take it easy. If I go where you'll teach?'

She only looked at him. He continued, 'That was only a joke. But I'll tell you something serious now. I'll tell you why I'm in UNE, and I ain't no university student. I joined UNE from the outside because I ain't making no joke, I against the Government because the Government against me. You could sell me out to your Secret Police. I against the Government because Brazil is too much of a damn rich country to have so many poverty-stricken people around. I mean you have people all over the place sleeping on the pavement, begging – it's sickening. And students there fighting like hell for these people, man. But what's happening to them? And as you all could see, here the poor man is the black man. As a black man I'll go down fighting for the black man. That's why I'm with the students. That's why I'm with UNE.'

Marisa and Alvin were both silent. Alvin wanted to keep on Marisa's side so he didn't want to say anything to support Mac.

Mac said, 'I could talk for hours on this.'

Marisa smiled quietly: 'Well don't talk for hours because Mr Alvin cannot stay and listen to us.'

'That's right. We can't take up his whole morning. Marisa, about that job – you finish talk?'

'There is nothing else,' she said.

'Well, okay, when you ready we'll go.'

'If you are ready we can go.'

They got up, Marisa and Alvin glanced at each other. Mac said, 'I must come back here and have a good talk. Not just about politics. I want some tourist brochures to put up in the school. And I want some magazines and newspapers and so on. You have any films on Trinidad?'

'Yes, but you'll have to see the boss for that.'

'Okay. I'll come back. We'll arrange something.'

'Okay, then. *Ciao!*'

'*Ciao*,' Mac replied. And Marisa gave Alvin a long look and said '*Ciao*.'

As soon as Alvin came back from the door the new girl said, 'What is his name?'

'Mac.'

'He is a member of UNE?'

'I heard him say something like that. You know about UNE?'

She laughed. 'I am in UNE,' she said.

Oh.' Alvin was surprised. It was the first time he was speaking to this girl. She seemed pleasant enough. What she said was quite interesting. He said, 'I must tell Mac about that. I'm sure he didn't realise you was in it. You never saw him at meetings?'

'No.'

I'll tell him you in UNE too.'

21

When Marisa returned to the trade office alone on the Friday she sat quietly down in one of the visitors' chairs, waiting. It was only half an hour before the office was due to close and she didn't want to disturb Alvin. But Vera went in and told him she was there.

Alvin was nervous and overjoyed. He came out and greeted her and when he went back into his office he came out again every few minutes to see that she was all right. And he kept looking at the clock to see how time was going.

Marisa felt embarrassed about Vera and about the new girl and so she kept very quiet. She felt that they knew something was happening. She avoided looking their way.

Alvin was sitting at his desk but he could hardly work. He had not believed Marisa would come alone and so he had not set much store on it. Now he kept thinking of what could happen when everybody was gone. He did not want to think of that yet. He knew Marisa a little and he did not want to build up any hopes of being familiar with her. He heard footsteps now and as he looked up, Marisa said, 'Hello.'

'Oh, hello, Mar.'

'Just looking at your office.'

'All right. But look out – the boss—'

'Your boss, he is gone.'

'He's gone? You sure? Mr Wilkes?' It was still ten minutes to four.

'Yes.'

'Good. He saw you?'

'He passed beside me and he went out.'

Alvin came out of his room and went across to Vera. Vera was clearing up her desk and on the point of leaving and that alone was confirmation that Mr Wilkes was gone. He said to himself, 'I didn't see at all.'

The new girl said, 'He just left.'

Vera, who wanted to give the impression that she, too, knew some English, said, 'What?'

Alvin said, 'Mr Wilkes.'

'He go already,' Vera said.

She looked round her shoulder at the new girl, and she said, meaningfully, 'She and me – soon we go too.'

Alvin laughed.

'Vera added, 'And Dona Ana – she go now.'

'I too,' Alvin said.

'You, no. You go—' And she pointed to Alvin's room where Marisa was. Both herself and the new girl nearly choked for laughing.

A few minutes later Alvin and Marisa were alone in the trade office. Alvin did not completely finish his chores yet and he let her sit on a chair in front of his desk. She could see that he was nervous and that his hands were unsteady and she knew that it was because of her.

After a few minutes he stopped working because he could not concentrate. He put down the papers, got up, and went round to her chair. He suddenly put his hand around her neck.

Both their hearts were thumping. She gently removed his hand.

'I think the world of you,' he said, breathing heavily.

'Well like that behave,' she said. 'Be a good boy.'

'Mar, I love you.' he said, 'I mean, you realise that?'

She feigned surprise: 'So like that? I must to tell you this. We girls. We girls in the Brazil. Are very strange. We do not like this – how you say it? You say you like me. Well perhaps I like you, too. But let us take time, no?'

Alvin looked at her and he felt cheated. She had come all the way from Tijuca to meet him, and although he felt that she was not going to be too soft to him he did not expect her to be so rigid. He felt hurt in a way but he knew that she was a fine girl and he could have no quarrel with her. All he had to do was to bide his time. They sat looking at each other and after a while he spoke.

'So Mar, you are disappointed in me?'

'A little bit.'

'Why.'

'You are bad. *Juizo.*'

He laughed. 'What's *"juizo"*?'

'It is what you don't have. It means "judgement". I thought you knew Portuguese.'

'"Judgement?" I wouldn't say it's judgement. It's more like "be careful".'

'Well you be careful,' she said.

Alvin laughed.

She said. 'I have to get back to Tijuca for six o'clock. To teach.'

Alvin looked at his watch. It was already a quarter past four. He said, 'We have bags of time. Let's take a little stroll, and afterwards I'll put you in a taxi.'

'What is a "stroll"?'

'It means a walk. I thought you knew English. Let's walk out to the beach, across here. Straight out to the beach, at the *enseada.*'

'All right.'

'Let me lock up the office and then we'll go.'

They went downstairs in the lift and they crossed Praia das Americas and then they walked down to the little park where there were benches to sit on. That was around the statue of Almirante Barroso. They did not sit in the park. They walked across the park, slowly, close to each other, and Alvin was thinking of taking her hand, but he was hesitant. Soon after the park they were on the pavement of the busy Praia do Flamengo and here Alvin took her hand to cross the street. They ran across. When they got to the other side he did not let go her hand.

His heart was racing. They looked at each other but did not say anything. Now after crossing a broad strip of ground they came to the *aterro,* and after getting past that there was not much more to walk to get to the beach.

It was still very hot and the beach of the *Enseada da Gloria* was crowded with bathers. Fringing the beach were several young coconut trees and the white shoreline formed a semi-circle. Alvin looked for a clean piece of wood and put it down for Marisa to sit. He himself sat down on the sand.

She said, 'Here it is very nice.'

'Like you.' He was looking into her face.

'You boys from Trinidad talk too much nonsense.'

'It's the truth, Mar.'

'Well, don't say it.' She put her finger on his lips and he was smiling up at her. She thought, 'You are a wonderful boy.' But she did not say anything.

For a moment Marisa looked at the bathers in the sea and then she lifted her eyes to the great expanse of blue water that was the Baía de Guanabara. The Baía da Guanabara seemed to sweep into the land, and beyond it, in the distance, were the hazy outlines of mountains.

She said, 'That over there – that is the Niteroi over there?'

'Yes, in the centre is Niteroi, and way out at the tip is Cabo Frio.'

'And where would the Petropolis be?'

'Petropolis is to the left there, look,' Alvin pointed. 'You see where those white clouds are in the hills? That is Petropolis.'

'You know very well the Estado do Rio.'

'I know all Rio. Not only the state but the city itself. I mean all Guanabara. I'm not Brazilian but I could still show a bit of Rio to Brazilians.' He looked at her and laughed.

She said, 'It is a shame for me. Here I like very much. It is *bacana.*'

'You never came here before?'

'No.' It is a shame. I know so little of the Brazil.'

'Anyway, don't worry, because you are really *Americana.*'

'I am Brazil. I want to be Brazil.' She said this almost fiercely.

'All right, all right, you are *Brasileira.*'

'I see you want to practice your Portuguese? Let us talk Portuguese.'

'No, we could talk English. It's okay with me.'

She looked around her. 'I like here very much.'

'You said you never came to this beach?'

'Never.'

'I come here all the time.'

'Here is where you bring your girls?'

'Girls? I don't know any girls.'

'That is true. I can see on your face that you don't know any girls.'

'You don't believe me?'

'Yes, I believe you,' she said, a look of mockery on her face.

And then her gaiety seemed to change completely, and she said, 'Alvin, what really you think of me?'

He sat up. 'What you mean? I like you. I told you already over in the Trade Office. I'm really serious about you, Mar.'

'But you think I am not a nice girl?'

'What make you feel so? I never said that. I only wanted to ask you—'

'What?'

'About Craig.'

'All right. Ask me.'

'What about you and Craig?'

'Craig, he was just a friend.'

'Nothing more?'

'Nothing more.'

'But he was a good friend?'

'*Claro.*'

'But. you weren't interested in him? You know what I mean.'

'No.'

'You answering short and sweet.'

She chuckled and looked at him.

He said, 'All right You didn't believe me a while ago but I believe you now.'

'But I tell you the truth *que dens me mata!*'

'No, don't make any oath in Portuguese because I wouldn't believe you.'

'In English I don't feel sincere. How you say it in English?'

'We just say "so help me God!" but don't bother because I believe you already. I was only making a joke, girl. If you fooling me you fooling yourself.' She did not understand that last part but she did not speak. She just looked at him.

He, too, was looking at her and now he felt as if the devil came into him and he threw his arms about her neck and pressed her towards him. She stiffened. He eased up and as he tried to kiss her she pulled herself away. She said, 'Alvin stop! *Pára*. There are people—'

'To hell with people!'

'*Pára!*' she said, and fended him off, holding both his hands. She was breathing fast. Then she said softly, 'There will be plenty of time.'

'True, true?' he said, panting.

'Yes.'

He let her go. He said, 'What is Mac to you.'

She was taken aback. 'You are jealous even of Mac?'

'So can't I ask?'

'You know that Mac is a married man.'

'So what's that! That is something too?'

'I suppose all men are that way. There is nothing – how you say it? – sacred. Anyway, there" is no reason to be jealous of Mac.'

'When I called for him some girl answered. That's his wife, Mar?'

'Perhaps, because she is always there. She came to your place with us that first day.'

'Oh yes, I remember. A white girl.'

'Yes. But Mac loves black people.' She giggled, looking at Alvin.

Alvin smiled and shook his head but he did not say anything. After a few moments he said, 'This Mac seems to be a nice feller but he's so bitter.'

'Bitter, yes. He is very, very. But it is only political. I teach in his school for two years and I can say he is a very good person.'

Alvin was quiet for a few moments, then he said, 'So Marisa, you don't have any boy-friend at all. I'd like to know, you know, because I can't stand any competition.'

She smiled at him.

'You smiling? You think I believe a girl like you ain't have anybody hanging around? Somebody must be interested.'

'Interested, *claro*. There are many men interested.'

He just stared at her.

She said, 'Jealous?'

'Yes.'

'Poor Alvin. There are many men interested but me, no. You only. Okay now? You feel well? Tell me, you will not be going back to Trinidad.'

'Me? I'm here for keeps. I could guarantee that.'

She turned to him: 'It is not possible. You work with the Government.'

'I'm here for keeps. After I finish my term here I'm free.'

Inside her there was a feeling of quiet happiness. She said, 'I want to know all about this.'

'I'll tell you.'

He turned round as though he were going to explain, then he suddenly held her and pulled her over to him and he tried to kiss her. She struggled but he found her lips, and when he released her she wrested herself away and she took up her handbag, got up, and walked off. He hurried off after her, putting his hand on her shoulder. He said, 'I'm sorry, Mar, believe me, I don't know what came over me. Oh God, don't get vexed, please.'

'I am not vexed,' she said softly.

22

Towards the end of the following week the new girl approached Alvin. She said: 'That friend of yours – I am thinking I saw him at a UNE meeting.'

'Which friend?'

'The friend who came here some time. He is *bonito*. You don't know? You said he was political.'

'Oh, you mean Mac. You saw him at a UNE meeting?'

'I am sure it was he that I saw at our meeting.'

'That's quite likely. Why didn't you ask him?'

'I could not. I was with officials and he was far, and, you see, there was many people.'

'You said you are an official – what sort of things you do?'

'I don't like to talk about this. People are so afraid of UNE.' She talked in a subdued tone of voice and all the time she was watching to see his reaction.

'That's true. The girl who came here with Mac – you remember? That girl said so.'

'What she said?'

'That UNE is powerful.'

'And that it is communist?'

'Yes.'

She gave a sneering sort of laugh. There was disdain but there was uneasiness in it too. She said: 'These people are so scared about communism. Everybody is so scared. I am doing this job here in your trade office because it is easy for me and it is good practise for my English, but if Mr Wilkes knows that I am in UNE I will have to leave right away. I know. These people are so afraid.'

'Wilkes is reasonable.'

'Reasonable? I know these diplomats. They are not themselves. I know these diplomats because my father was one.' 'Your father was a diplomat? Oh, yes, Mr Wilkes said so.'

'That is right.'

'Anyway, Wilkes is only a civil servant.'

'Oh, yes, but a trade office is nearly to an embassy. It is only a step away. *Comércio* is very important to these countries – not people, *comércio*.' She said this with some irony. 'I know these people.'

'Anyway, you could trust me because Wilkes wouldn't hear anything from me. But wait – I know you came in as a translator but how come your English is so good? You are not Brazilian?'

'With a name like "Ilka"?' she laughed. 'No, I was born in Germany. But my father, he was the German Ambassador and I have lived all over the world.'

'Oh, I see. Your father was German Ambassador. I think you said so before, but it didn't sink in.'

'That's why I know them so well.'

'You spent some time in England?'

'Many years. That is why my English is so – well, not good. It used to be very good. Perfect.'

'That's funny, the girl who came here with Mac her English is perfect too, like—'

'I heard her English.'

'And she is Brazilian, you know.'

'I could tell by her accent, and she is talking American English.'

'Well she was in America. She spent five years in America when she was small. I think she was born there. The fantastic thing is she ain't forget anything. The father talk English too, and they keep it up.'

'That's good. What is she to Mac?'

'Mac has a little school of English and she teaches for him. But apart from that they are friends. When she comes back here you two must talk.'

'She wouldn't like me. She is scared about communists.'

'Look, don't judge her yet. I could tell you about this girl. She is the nicest, simplest person you'll ever meet. She couldn't care less if you are communist – or whatever you are.'

'In this world you have to care.'

'Well, some people—' Ilka made a gesture to him and at the same time Alvin saw Vera emerge from Mr Wilkes' office and he stopped talking. Vera brought something for Ilka to translate and

Ilka took it and went over to her desk. She muttered to Alvin in Portuguese that she would talk to him again.

At midday, after Mr Wilkes had left, and after both Vera and Dona Ana had left, Alvin saw Ilka sitting at her desk and walked over to her. Ilka had been designing posters for UNE and when she saw Alvin she slipped magazines over them. Alvin said, 'You aren't going home for lunch?'

'Today I am staying in to look at something.'

'Tell me – you in Brazil a long time?'

'Yes, we came here when I was twelve and my father had two terms here. So we are now here six years. Before that we was in Madrid and before that, in London.'

'Oh, yes? And your family is still here?'

She shook her head. 'My father went but I stayed. I have all my friends in Brazil I didn't want to leave when my parents went off.'

'What you think of Brazil, really. You like here?'

'But *claro.* I like very much this place. I feel this country as my own country. The Rio is *bacana* but I like especially the people. But the Government, it is terrible. You have a long time here?'

'Two years.'

'This *ditadura* – how you say in English—'

'Dictatorship.'

'Yes, this dictatorship is terrible. The poverty in the *favelas* and *morros* you cannot believe. And the ignorance! It is the whole system. All over America Latina it is bad but here it is the worse. The rich people want this. They want to keep the *povo*—'

She paused. Alvin said, 'Masses. *Povo* is masses.'

'They want to keep the masses down underneath. They want to crush the people. And when we protest they say it is subversion. But the UNE have to care. The UNE have to fight. That is what it is fighting.'

She got all worked up and red in the face. Alvin did not want her to go on and he looked at his watch to distract her and he said, 'What! Half past twelve already?' He said this sincerely, in a way. He wanted to leave her now but it was too late to go away for lunch. He said, 'I think I'd better fast today, like you. Anyway, you stayed back to look at something so I'd better leave you alone.'

'No, it's all right. I cannot do much work now.'

'So sorry.'

'No, It is all right. Our converse was good.'

He asked her in Portuguese what she had been doing at the university, and that set them off speaking Portuguguese and they carried on the conversation until it was one o'clock.

As soon as Dona Ana and Vera appeared he switched to English so they wouldn't understand. She said now, 'Your Portuguese is good.'

'Perhaps not bad for a foreigner. But you talk Portuguese just like you any other Brazilian.'

She retorted, 'But I am just like any other Brazilian, no?'

'I was talking about your accent. Just that.'

The door was pushed open again and this time it was Mr Wilkes who entered. When Ilka spotted him she pulled magazines over the poster. But it was already covered and as she flicked the magazines she uncovered the words: UNE CONTINUA.

23

On Friday evening Alvin went down to Praça Saens Pena to meet Marisa. He had been telephoning her all through the week and she had arranged to meet him on Friday after class. She had said that nine in the evening was too late for her but he had insisted. Now, at nine, he was in the praça waiting.

He did not have to wait long. The clock at the lower end of the praça had just pointed to nine when Marisa arrived She had seen Alvin from a long way off and now she walked straight up to him.

She said, 'Hello, *como vai*.' She was excited. 'How is everything?'

He answered in Portuguese.

'Very well. You are Brazilian boy, now. You do not speak the English any more.'

'You spoke to me in Portuguese. You said, *'Como vai'*'

He dressed round for her to sit but she kept standing. She looked animated. She said, 'Okay, everyone know that *"como vai"* is "how you go", so I say that.' You don't look to go very well. What about the trade office?'

'It's still there. Same place. Mar, you know your English is not so good today at all?'

'Why do you say so?'

'I don't know. You aren't sounding as good as usual. The accent is heavy, and – I don't know.'

'It is because I was talking the Portuguese all day. To teach I have to talk Portuguese. Even with Mac I am talking Portuguese. That is no good for me.'

'Oh, you talk Portuguese with Mac but with me it's only English!'

'I like to talk English with you to improve my English. I don't like so well the English of Mac. There are eighty million people in the Brazil and you can talk Portuguese with all of them, but excuse me please and let me talk English alone with you.'

'I don't mind at all. But I only hope you don't like me just for

English.'

She laughed. 'That's funny.' Now she rested down a few books and sat down beside him on the bench.

'I know it sounds funny but tell me the truth.'

'What truth? I like English very much, but not in the same way I like you.'

He felt thrilled. 'I don't believe you. Why you liked Craig?'

'Craig? He was the friend of Mac. I liked to speak with him for his English, too, but also because he was a friend of Mac.'

They were sitting right up beside each other. Alvin did not grab her now as he was so confident. He threw an arm around her neck.

She said, 'Do not do that here. Here there are many people who know me.'

He took his hand away. 'You bothering with people? You are a big woman, can't you have a boy-friend?'

'Yes, but like this, no.' She took his hand in hers. 'Do not get *zangado*.'

'Mar, the English word is "angry". Your English is shaky today, eh? How come you're teaching English and making so many simple mistakes?'

'I don't know.' She felt very humiliated.

He looked at her face and chuckled. 'Don't worry,' he said, 'Sometimes it's like hell for even me to speak good English.'

Although it was well after nine p.m. there were a lot of people in the praça. There were not many sitting on the benches, but there were groups standing about in the praça, some walking around it on the pavement, and there were people passing through the square from one side to the other. Also, there were still nursemaids and parents and children down at the playground end. Over at the nearby fountain there was a jet of water spraying from one side of the pool to the other, and sitting looking at this Marisa fell silent. She was remembering past evenings here with Craig.

After a little while Alvin noticed her quietness and said:

'You worried about something?'

'No.'

'Don't worry about what I said just now. About your English. I was more making a joke.'

'I know.' Then she looked towards him, 'How is the trade office?'

'Oh well, you know. I told you about this new girl?'

'How about her?'

Alvin just shrugged.

'Marisa, you take everything so easy, I wish I was you. Now, this girl – I get to know a little more about her. She is really nice, pleasant, and she is supposed to be the daughter of a diplomat, and all that. And she isn't at all vain – you know what "vain" is? – Well she's all right, but I can't help feeling that it's you who should be there instead of she.'

'Mac, too, feel so. Mac is very angry about her. But it is time to forget it. Anyway, your boss choose her. And maybe the girl is good.'

'She *is* good, you could believe me. But I think Mac doesn't like her not only because you didn't get the job. You see, Mac is a revolutionary and—'

'Mac is not revolutionary, he is crazy.'

Alvin laughed. 'Maybe he's crazy – I don't know about that. But the truth is, Mac really feels for black people and he wants them to get on. He is one of those people who feels strongly. There are people like that in the world, let's face it. Mac is obsessed with this and I admire him. But ideology for me is somehow something different. I don't know what is communism, or capitalism, or facism. To me what matter is not ideology, but as the fellow said – I don't know who it is – what matters is how you treat your fellow men. So on this politics side I'm not so interested. But if I have to fight, of course I'm fighting with Mac. This whole question is so – I don't know. Now I was going to say this: when I look at a lovely, elegant, black girl like you, you know how proud I feel? You'll never know. I'm not giving you basket—'

'What?'

'Okay, forget it. "Basket" is just "flattery". Anyway, now I'm not going to criticise you, but it seems to me as if you believe everything is right with Brazil.'

She looked at him sharply. 'No, no, no. This is wrong, I do not feel so.'

'Well I think you give that impression.'

'Because you listen to Mac, that is why. But it is not so. I tell Mac all the time that I know that colour prejudice exists in the Brazil. But I hear my father talk about America do Norte and I know that

the Brazil is a very different country. I read about other places and I
know that the Brazil is one of the best countries in the world. There
are many things wrong, I know. But Mac keeps talking about
revolution. He is crazy. In revolution they fight and kill. You do not
change anything by revolution.'

'Really? I'm not so sure. But I'll agree with you that revolution
is not the only way, and that's why I'm against it. And after all, if
there are many other good things, they might go too. But anyway,
let's leave that. Something I wanted to ask you; Mac knows about
you and me?'

She looked at him. 'I do not understand.'

'I mean I was wondering if Mac knows that I'm going after
you. He ever said anything?'

'No, why?'

'Well he knew you and Craig were going good and—'

'Going good?' She chuckled. 'Poor Alvin. Anyway, Mac has so
many things to do, do you expect him to notice us?'

There were a few moments of silence. Then Alvin said: 'He is a
boy I have a lot of admiration for. He's a boy I like.'

'I know that.'

'He's always making joke but he is a very serious chap.'

She listened to him smiling.

'What you so amused about?'

'No reason.'

She was smiling because she realised how easily Alvin had been
influenced by Mac. Alvin was worried and embarrased about Mac
knowing about them but she knew that Mac would have liked to be
in the same position that Alvin was in now. Since Alvin had a great
admiration for Mac and obviously saw him as a saint, she would not
disillusion him. Thinking of "saint" she said now. 'You are of what
religion?'

'Catholic.'

'I also.' She was pleased. 'Mac said most people in Trinidad are
Roman Catholics.'

'Among the Christians, yes. You believe in religion?'

'Most times. You?'

'Sometimes I believe. At this moment *you* are my religion. I
believe in you.' He was still holding her hand and as he said that he

threw the arm around her neck and pulled her to him. She did not struggle, and he kissed her, and they remained long in an embrace.

'Afterwards he said, Marisa, this is no joke. I love you bad and I want you.'

'I know.'

'Is that possible? You know what I'm talking about.'

'*Claro*, it is possible. When you get married to me.'

'But you know I'll get married to you.'

'When?'

'I could get married to you tomorrow, because I want to. But we'll have to wait a little bit.'

'All right, I know', She squeezed his hand. 'So you will wait a little bit.' She looked at him and chuckled.

'Girl this thing about our getting married. We'll talk about when, eh?'

'All right.'

He kissed her again, and then they both sat there silently, Marisa leaning her head on his shoulder. She could not see the clock of the praça but it must have been past ten and she began to think about going home. She was feeling uneasy about her parents. She could not possibly tell them why she was late. Not until they knew Alvin.

'I have to invite you home,' she said now.

'Any time. If you like, tonight.'

'No, not tonight. You are crazy, like Mac.'

They laughed.

Now, most of the people at the playground end of the praça had disappeared, but there was still a lot of activity about. On all sides of the praça there were people walking on the pavements.

Alvin said, 'You want to walk round the square a little?'

She said in Portuguese that she was thinking of going home.

'Talk English. I like to hear your funny accent in English.'

'And I like to hear your funny Portuguese.'

They both laughed.

Alvin said, 'Get up. Let's walk round the square.'

'Okay. Just once, and I have to go home.'

They joined the groups walking around the praça. The crowds were mainly of courting couples and separate groups of boys and girls. The boys were walking behind the girls and teasing them, and the girls, although they seemed to be enjoying it, were feigning anger.

Alvin said, 'After this I'll walk you home eh, Mar?'

'No, not yet.'

He had his arm around her waist and she was very stiff.

'You are still afraid of people seeing you?'

'A little.'

'No one ain't have time with us,' he said. 'Like what you said about Mac. In any case, one could be lonely in a crowd – you ever hear that saying?'

'No, but it sounds good.'

'I'm a poet tonight,' he said.

They were about half-way round the praça. From the Rua Conde de Bonfim they had borne left along the Rua General Roca, and then down the Rua Saens Pena, and now they were back again in the Rua Conde de Bonfim. They turned into the Rua General Roca again, and when Alvin looked at the dark stretch of the Rua General Roca beyond the praça, he said, 'Down there is too dark. I'll walk you down. It could be dangerous walking down there alone.'

'It could be dangerous walking down there with you,' she said. They laughed. Then she said, 'Alvin, no please, not now. But I will invite you home very soon.'

'The sooner the better.'

'All right. I will see you. I will ring you on Monday because on weekends I am with my family. Okay? *Ciao!*'

'*Ciao!*'

He stood there watching her until she disappeared in the darkness.

24

Not many days afterwards a policeman came into Praça Saens Pena and sat down on one of the benches on the side of Rua Saens Pena. To his left and far ahead near the Rua Conde de Bonfim, was a clump of hedge, and straight in front of him was the fountain jetting out water. In the little space between the clump of hedge and the fountain the gateway to Mac's school was in full view.

The policeman looked at his watch, which was showing five minutes to nine, and he kept his eyes on the entrance of Mac's school. When it was dead on nine p.m. he watched the dozens of students surge out onto the pavement.

He sat back now and waited. And sure enough the young woman came into the praça. She looked around, then she sat down in her usual seat near the middle of the praça. He watched her for a few minutes as she sat alone, and seeing that her companion did not turn up he got up and started to walk in her direction. As he walked along the concrete footpath he saw her companion arrive and sit down next to her. He went on walking and as he passed them he gazed fixedly at her for a moment. He then went to the other side of the praça and sat down looking at her.

Alvin said, 'That policeman who just passed. You saw how he looked at you? Who is he?'

'I do not know.'

'I find he's always in the square at this time.'

'He is always here. And he is always looking at me. I do not know if it is a thing to do with UNE.'

'UNE? It shouldn't be. You don't mix up yourself with UNE.'

She looked at him, 'Mac told you about the demonstration?'

'Oh, you mean that thing with the university – what they call *passeata?*'

'Yes.'

'Yes, I know about it.'

'I am a little frightened about this policeman. He looks at me a lot. I did not want to tell you anything, but you saw.'

'Forget him,' Alvin said. He fell silent. The policeman's figure seemed like a ghost against the passing cars of the Rua Conde de Bonfim. Alvin kept his eyes on him. He said, 'One night when I got here before you I saw a feller like him sitting on the other side, over there. It looked as if he was watching Mac's school.'

'It has perhaps to do with the *passeata*.'

'You mean they already know Mac with this political business, and knowing that you work there—'

'Yes.'

'That place is not the best place to work.'

'I don't know. Really, I do not know if they know Mac. The police here knows of everything.'

'You have to watch this. Something up. Something definitely up.'

The two sat there, arm in arm, and they were very pensive. Although they shifted the conversation to other things, the thought of the policeman dominated their minds.

When they got up to go, Alvin asked, 'When is the *passeata* again?'

'Next month. The twentyfourth.'

'How you think it will pass?'

'It will be big. The papers said students from all Brazilian universities will join it. That alone will make them join it. These people are crazy.'

'But there must be something wrong with Brazil why a thing like this could catch on so. I mean, there must be something that cause the young people to make so much trouble.'

'It is not in general the young people, it is only the students. The students they have a problem – university places. But it is not a big problem because they already themselves have places. But it is the communists who are rushing to make a problem. They want to overthrow the Government. It is wicked.'

'What? The Government?'

She did not understand. 'What?'

He laughed. 'I'm only making a joke.' Then he turned to her seriously and whispered: 'What about Mac – he's a communist?'

She glanced around her. 'Mac, no. But they are using him.'

'I was going to ask you about Ilka but you don't know Ilka.'

'I know a little about her.'

'What about her?'

She appeared not to hear.

'She's a communist?'

'Why you ask?'

'Because Vera told me she's a communist.'

'Your boss, he reads the papers?'

'He doesn't know Portuguese so well, you know. In fact, Ilka has to translate everything for him.'

Marisa wanted to laugh but she could not. She said, 'I told you before, be very careful about the Ilka. But I do not know if she is a communist.'

'It's all right. We don't have any Government secrets in the trade office. But this whole question of communism. I don't know. It might depend on how you see the world. But anyway, what I was going to say was, you be damn careful with the police, eh?'

'I will be all right. If they question me I do not know anything.'

'But please try and avoid any kind of questioning. Another thing, if the police knows Ilka, perhaps they watching the trade office.'

To keep him calm, Marisa said, 'I do not think they know the Ilka. The important ones like Vladimir Palmyra, yes. But not the Ilka.'

'Who is Vladimir Palmyra?'

'He is the President of UNE.'

'Anyway, try and avoid any questioning, eh? Because that might involve me, and I don't want to get involved.'

'*Claro.*'

Long before they got up to go the policeman had left. Now he was standing on the pavement and the junction of Rua Saens Pena with Rua General Roca. He watched Alvin and Marisa as they stood up at the far end of the Rua Saens Pena, and he saw when they embraced, and when Alvin came back and walked up the road. Now his eyes followed Marisa. There was a lamp post beside him and as he saw her coming up the Rua Saens Pena and into the Rua General Roca he stood back behind the lamp post to watch her pass.

Marisa was very nervous and at every few steps she looked

around to see if she was being watched. Now she looked into the praça but she did not see the policeman. She looked at the next side by the cinema and coffee shop. When she reached the junction and looked towards the Rua Conde de Bonfim she jumped. There was the policeman standing just beside her.

'*Boa noite*,' he said, smiling. '*Bootifool lorve.*'

She turned her head away. He kept beside her, trying to speak English to her, but she flashed a hostile look at him and crossed the street to the other side. Then she breathed out a sigh of relief. This was just a man who was infatuated with her. This was nothing political and Mac had nothing to do with it. She walked home feeling happy.

25

The next evening Marisa went to classes early just to tell Mac about the policeman. Mac listened to her patiently, and at the end he said, 'You could fool yourself but I wouldn't fool you. You nice, I mean, you attractive, everybody know that, but he wasn't looking at you because you attractive. And he didn't say 'good night' because he wanted to chat you down. They know you teaching with me and they know I'm involved with this *passeata*.'

'I at first thought so but it is not.'

Mac laughed mockingly and then he shook his head. He said, 'You think that surprise me? I always tell you how naive you is and you don't believe me. You believe that Brazil is the best country, and the prejudice is only economic and so on. Now you believe that this policeman was looking at you because he like you. I think the only time you'll believe what I saying is when police swoop on the school and arrest me.'

'*Meu deus*! Mac, don't speak like that.'

'It's all right, what you worried about? Alvin could always find you a job in the trade office. Especially if they arrest Ilka too.'

'I am not worried about the job I am worried about you. If they arrest you and put you in jail you will rot there in jail.'

'And so what?'

'They will say that you are a communist.'

'But a lot of people already say that. So what? If I'm a communist, so what?'

She was visibly distressed. 'You could not be a communist; you are one of the best people I know.'

Mac laughed. Then he said, 'Look, Mar, don't get in a state. One thing I want to say. I could figure you out and there is only one word to describe you – brainwashed. But let's leave that. The thing is, I wouldn't like them to arrest me, but I ain't going to stop. What UNE stands for is bigger than me or Ilka. In fact, I can't describe it.

Let them arrest me when they ready. I'm not going to hide nowhere. It's the future of black people at stake.'

She turned to him sharply, 'You always say that. UNE is not black people. UNE is university students and few black people could go to university.'

'That is exactly what we want to change.'

'That is what *you* want to change, not the UNE. UNE is not worried of black people.'

'So say Mar.'

'We blacks are poor. UNE is white people and rich people.'

'So you are saying what I always say. That this thing about equality here is nonsense. You agreeing with me that we have two Brazils – rich and poor, black and white?'

'That is true always here. I will not deny it. But I believe that everybody are friends, not like in *Estados Unidos*. We will be making change, but I do not believe we need a revolution and fighting and killing.'

'It will have to have a revolution, girl. You could jump high you could jump low but there will be revolution.'

'But even if UNE brings revolution who you think it will help? The rich only want things for themselves.'

Mac smiled at her. 'Mac know that. But this time it will be different, girl. This is people out for change. You'll see a new Brazil. This is what *I* fighting for. I'll give my blood, girl!'

She was already agitated, and hearing blood now she became even more so. She said, 'Mac, you are brave but I am afraid.'

'Don't be afraid for me.'

Students were beginning to come in. Some of them lingered to hear Mac and Marisa talk English before filtering into their classrooms.

Mac said, 'Anyway, we must talk some other time, I think we getting to see eye to eye somehow. Inside, we feel the same way. And you coming round. You getting the message.'

'I hope *you* will get the message,' she said.

26

Early the next week Mac went to the trade office and after greeting the two girls, he said to Alvin, 'I hear you controlling U N E?'

'Me?'

Looking towards Ilka, he said, 'Well you have the key girl here.'

They laughed. Ilka said, 'You are the Mac?'

'In person. I've been seeing you at meetings but you don't know me.'

'No,' she said. 'But I heard you are in U N E. I am glad to meet you. Thank you for giving support to U N E.'

'Giving support to U N E ? Girl I have a wife and children to support?'

Alvin and Mac burst out laughing. Alvin said to Ilka, 'This man is always making fun — don't mind him.'

Ilka was looking at Mac. Mac said, 'Well, to be serious, I am in U N E, though under false pretences. Because I'm not even a student. Let's say I believe in the cause.'

'Thank you very much. Most people think that the U N E is for only university students. The problem in Brazil is not only for university students.'

'That's so true.'

'Alvin said that you have a school of English.'

'Yes I have a little school at Saens Pens.'

'That is good. You can create a lot of impression through a school. You can get your students to join the *passeata*.'

'Those students of mine? Girl those people will need a lot of waking up.'

'Yes, I know. Here too.' She looked sidelong at Alvin.

Alvin said, 'I already explain that I am a Government man. For better or for worse. I can't get myself involved.'

Ilka said, 'It is true but I wasn't thinking about you alone. The whole country needs waking up.'. She looked outside and now there was no smile on her face. 'We will shake them up,' she said. 'We will bring out a million for the *passeata.'*

Mac looked at her.

She turned to him, 'That is no joke. We will get people from all over Brazil. We will—'

Mr Wilkes came into the room. Although he seemed very much in a hurry he said a very pleasant 'good morning' to Mac. He handed over a folder to Alvin, exchanged a few words with him, and went out again.

Mac said, 'At least Wilkes could be civil.'

Alvin said, 'He's not a bad feller, really. I would call him a nice feller.' He glanced up at Ilka.

Ilka did not speak. But she said to herself, 'All these nice fellers will have to be put away. All these nive Government boys.' She sadi to Mac, 'Well, it is good to see you. I will go over to my desk but I will hope to see you before you go.'

'Oh, sure,' Mac said.

Mr Wilkes busied himself in his office, and presently he dashed over to Alvin again, then he went back to his office for his jacket, and he soon disappeared. Mac walked over to Ilka's desk. When she saw him coming she drew a chair for him to sit down. She said now, 'It is good that you are in U N E.'

'I should say that I'm with U N E rather than in U N E.'

'It is nice. U N E need all the people it could get. Especially for the *passeata* U N E want everybody.'

'I know.' He looked at her sitting there and had she not been talking like that he would never have thought she was a revolutionary. She was shapely, and she was wearing a tight-fitting crimson dress cut low around the neck. She had mascara on her eyelashes, and her lips were even redder than her dress.

Mac said, 'Listen, I hear you are organising the *passeata"*

'Yes'.

'You feel sure it will be a big success?'

She smiled. 'What I told you, you don't believe, no? We are going to put a million people on the street.' And she stressed again, 'A *million* people.'

'That sounds fantastic.'

'That sounds fantasy?'

'No, I said it sounds fantastic. It sounds great.'

'It is going to be great. It will be the biggest demonstration in the Brazil. U N E is in all the universities from Para — our state most north — to Rio Grande do Sul, in the South. Every, every state in the Brazil. A million people will be of the students alone. Then there will be friends and familia. I tell you it will be a day the Rio will never forget.'

'You make me feel so excited.'

'You understand now?'

'*Claro*.' He felt as if the blood was rushing up and down inside him.

'And naturally you will be there.'

'But Jesus Christ I will be in the thick of it. You don't know what this means to me — you really don't know! I have my whole heart in this thing.'

To hear him talk like that thrilled her. Her heart raced. She said, 'You are from the Trinidad but you really have fogo for the Brazil. You really have the fire.'

He was silent.

She said, 'I could see how deep you feel for the Brazil.'

'Right down. Deep down inside me.'

She said, 'It is odd. I am from Germany. Vladimir Palmyra is from Russia. Why is it that the foreigners risk more their blood?'

'But this is really strange. Vladimir, the President of U N E, is from Russia?'

'I am not sure but I believe that he was born there'.

Mac was thinking hard, and then he said, 'It doesn't really matter where you were born. I believe in John Donne. You ever hear about John Donne?'

'Oh, he was an Englishman of a long, long time.'

'That's right. He said: "No man is an island, entire of itself; every main is a part of the continent, a piece of the main." I find that so great.'

'*Nossa Senhora*, that is lovely. The English can always say these things.'

'And in that same part, that same thing, he said: "Every man's death diminisheth! me, because I am involved in mankind." Oh God girl, words, eh?'

She was so profoundly moved that all she said was, 'What's his name again?'

'John Donne.'

'He was a revolutionary?'

'He was a poet but *claro* those views would be revolutionary fro the big whigs.' He got up from the chair.

She said to him, 'I will like to see you again. I will like us to work together. Your feeling is the same as mine.'

'When can we meet?' He stood there looking at her. As he looked at her figure, sensual and inviting, his mind began thinking of all sorts of things besides politics.

'Anytime,' she said, 'I will be always glad.'

'I'll telephone you and perhaps we could see later.'

27

When June came talk of the *passeata* was sweeping the city. The students' union had its headquarters at the Universidade Pacheco of Rio de Janeiro, and there, the students were in open rebellion against their professors, and against the entire management, who wanted to stop the *passeata*.

Apart from the students almost everyone talked of the *passeata*. The city was full of disgruntled people. Housewives were against the Government because prices in the shops had gone up. Not only that but there was a water and electricity shortage in the city – possibly the result of sabotage. However, people were incensed. They talked openly of joining the *passeata*.

At this time the students' union was holding quick, clandestine meetings in various parts of the city. They called on the people to join the *passeata* and help crush the Government. They blamed the Government for what they called the alarming state of affairs in Brazil and said that the Government was bent on making the rich richer and the poor poorer. They pointed to the *favelas* in the hills around the city and asked what was being done. They talked about the forest-clad state of Amazonas and said that Brazil had one of the richest regions in the world while it remained one of the poorest countries in the world. They said that the Government preferred to rule by force and by clamping people in jail to silence them. They said that the Government was afraid to educate the masses, and that this was why there were so few state schools and so few university places. They attacked the Government on every side and said that the *passeata* was their last peaceful weapon to bring the Government to reason.

This atmosphere of unrest unsettled Marisa and now one evening when Alvin turned up in the praça to meet her, she said, 'This *passeata*, I am afraid. It seems that there will be really trouble'.

Alvin said, 'It will be a big thing. I could see that. Too many people are against the Government.'

'Without any truth at all. What do they want the Government to do? Make miracles? They want the *favelas* all removed at once. It is impossible.'

'People always seem to expect miracles. The Government will have it hard for this *passeata*'.

'And now the newspapers are giving much notice to the communists.'

'Well the papers publish to sell, you know. Not for your health. They know everybody is keen on the *passeata* so they building it up. And when a few of them get closed down by the Government, the students get even more publicity'.

'But these newspapers, they want to see fighting here?'

'They don't care.'

'But if these crazy people throw over the Government, then they will care. Because there will be no newspapers. The communists will ban them. The communists respect only their own views.'

They both remained quiet for a moment, distrubed. Then Alvin said, 'Things going from bad to worse. I told you Ilka went away last week?'

'When she was sick?'

'She said she was sick. I don't know. All I know is that she was doing more work for UNE than for us. And I had to keep everything quiet because if Wilkes knew, well ——. I just hinted to her what I noticed and the next day she said she had a headache and she went home. At first I thought it was genuine, but seeing that she ain't come back yet, well, I don't know.'

'She is not sick – she is working for the *passeata*.'

'Anyway, if she stays off much longer I'll have to tell Wilkes she left.'

'No. don't do that. Mac will know of it.'

'Look, if Wilkes let her go, you will be able to come in. Which should have been the case in the first place.'

'I don't want you to do that yet,' Marisa said. 'Mac will be very angry. If you don't see her in a few weeks then you could tell Mr. Wilkes about me.'

'You seem very concerned about Mac.'

She turned to him sharply. 'I work with him. I work with him for two years now.'

'But that ain't anything. That school is a bundle of trouble, you can't see? You go and get mixed up in that communist business.'

'I already told you Mac is not a communist.'

'You said you believed he wasn't – which is a different thing. You youtself say UNE is communist. If UNE is communist, he is.'

'What is communism,' Marisa asked.

Alvin looked at her, confused. She smiled. She said, I remember something about "It is not what you believe.... It is how you treat your fellow men...." Who said that?' She was chuckling.

'Okay, I said that.'

She said earnestly, 'Alvin, believe me if I tell you. Mac himself is good. He is a little crazy, but he is good. This change, it is because of the Ilka. Mac talks about revolution but I tell you I don't believe he is serious. But it is the Ilka. Now I tell you, the Ilka came to the school last week. They are loving. Loving, Yes, already. Do you believe Mac is serious? I say this because he says he is always supporting black people. But first, he married the Linda and now he is loving secretly the Ilka.'

'You sure they carrying on something?' Alvin was shocked.

'*Claro*. I see them.'

'Look, I don't like this thing at all. Man is a man-about-town and I don't want him to start on you. I don't like the idea of your working there.'

'Do not worry. But if the Ilka does not come back to the trade office you can speak for me.'

'I'll give her about a week more.'

'And what about you – there is news yet about your staying?'

'Not yet.'

'But there will be no trouble. Everybody gets a visa to stay in the Brazil.'

'Oh yes, I'll get it.'

Inside him he did not feel entirely confident that he would get it. The Brazilian authorities were taking a long time and wondered why. It was at these times that he felt close to Mac.

He said, 'As soon as I get the okay to stay here I'll come and visit your family – right?'

'Yes.'

'You are anxious for me to visit your home?'

28

A few evenings afterwards Marisa arrived at school early and said to Mac, 'Mac, I am thinking last night about that old man – Craig's uncle – on the Alto da Boa Vista. I feel sorry for him and perhaps he thinks we are angry because of Craig.'

'What made you remember him?'

'I don't know. I was just thinking of how Craig was silly that night, and I think of the old man.'

'And what made you think of Craig.'

'My white high-heeled shoes. I saw them at home. They were no good after that night.'

Mac shook his head, 'That boy is such a donkey. Anyway, I too does remember the old man. But I can't make the time to go up to see him now, you know. But I'll go up.'

'You feel you want to see him?'

'But of course? Why not? I don't have anything against the old man. One day we must go up the hill to see him. But it will have to be after the *passeata*.'

She was silent. She was standing up before her blackboard in her room and Mac was sitting on a desk close to her. They could hear a few early students outside chattering in Portuguese on the subject of English.

She said, 'Perhaps we could go to see him on one of the Sundays. You and me and that man at the trade office.'

'What man at the trade office. You mean your boyfriend!'

'What?'

'Look Mar, I know, but it's not my business. So you don't have to pretend. I always see you in the praça with him. But what you 'fraid for? You ain't have anything to hide.'

She said nothing but just looked at him.

Mac said, 'If you like him, you like him, that's all. You don't have to say, "That Trinidadian man". Get me?'

Marisa said, 'All right. So you want to know the truth.'

'I know the truth already.'

She laughed.

'Okay, perhaps we three could go up the hill to see Uncle. I'll welcome Alvin.'

'Uncle will be glad. To see another Trinidadian he will feel better.'

There was still a few minutes to go for classes to begin and Marisa said, 'Mac, I want to tell you something. I am sad.'

'About what?'

'I want to talk to you.'

'Shoot.'

'How is the Linda?'

'She's well. She's right there – you didn't see her?'

'It is not my business either, but—' She stopped.

'Go on. What you driving at?'

'I know what is happening. I think it is bad.'

'Yes, I know you know what is happening. And I know that it's I who have something to hide, but I ain't hiding a damn thing. So what! Anybody who want to know could know. Mar, I ain't have no satisfaction to give to nobody, but I'll talk to you because I like you. It's near time to teach now but as soon as I get a chance I'll tell you the situation. But as you could see, Linda ain't in nothing.'

'But she is your wife.'

'I know it's my wife. But Linda doesn't feel anything about what's happening in this country. At least, you argue, so you care. I mean, I don't agree with your views but at least you argue, but not Linda. What we did – Linda and I – was a big mistake.'

'Please don't say that.'

'But I say it. And it's the gospel truth. We shoulda never get married.'

'The mistake was when the Ilka came along.'

'Never. Mar you don't know. From the time I had a little talk with Ilka I knew she was my type. I could feel that she was my sister.'

'Not your sister – your wife, you mean.'

Mac could not help laughing. They were keeping their voices rather low now. Mac said, 'Marisa, you know you good for yourself? You is real trouble.'

'I am really sorry for the Linda.'

'I too. But I'm a man and Ilka is a damn attractive woman. She doesn't only have what it takes, Mar. Her heart is in the right place.'

They ended the conversation as the students began to trickle in. The clock in Marisa's classroom was dead on six. As Mac left Marisa to go over to his classroom he met Linda's eyes, glaring at him from the reception desk.

Just before lessons were over Mac peeped into Marisa's classroom and said, 'You could stay a little after class? To continue this talk?'

Marisa hesitated. 'Tonight?'

Mac said, 'He's coming to meet you?'

Marisa made a small nod.

'Okay then. Some other time.'

'But you can join us.'

'I don't want to, really.'

'Yes, please join us.'

'Okay, I'll see you after class.'

After classes Mac walked out to the praça with Marisa and there they met Alvin seated on a bench. Alvin looked very shamefaced and surprised that Mac should discover him there. Mac shook hands with him and then invited them to a nearby restaurant where they sat on tall stools, and he ordered *chope* beer for himself and Alvin, and fruit juice for Marisa. Then he ordered pizza pie for Alvin and Marisa. Now he turned to Alvin and said: 'So how the trade office going?'

'Not bad. Fair to fine.'

Alvin did not say anything more for he did not want to talk about the trade office. He did not want to talk about it, mainly because of the matter of Ilka. Mac was bound to know that at the moment she was not at the trade office. He was very sensitive to this and about Mac finding out about himself and Marisa. Mac, for his part, was quite easy. For one thing, the relationship between Marisa and Alvin was not new to him – only that he had not had much time to take note of it. But he felt it was not his business anyway. He turned to Alvin to make some fun. They talked, but Alvin remained subdued.

After the drinks arrived, Mac said, 'Well now, *senhorita*, let's hear about this Uncle business. When you want to go up the hill?'

'When is best for you. Any time.'

'Well you realise I can't do it now. Not until the twenty fourth of June.'

'It is all right. It does not have importance when we go. I only said it because it came to my mind.'

'Really, I have been thinking a hell of a lot about it. I like that old man.'

Alvin was looking at them questioningly. 'What's that?'

Marisa said, 'It is about the uncle of Craig.'

Mac said, 'Oh, he don't know about it yet? Mar, you ain't tell him about it.'

'It is only today I thought of it like that.'

Alvin looked towards Mac and Mac explained, 'It's about Craig's uncle. He is a very pleasant old man, but he's so lonely, and the man doesn't speak a word of Portuguese. When we went up to the Alto when Craig was going we promised to go back and look him up. And you see now Craig's gone we don't want him to feel we give him up. I didn't forget him, but I can't go up there now so I didn't worry Mar about it. But today Marisa mentioned it.'

'Oh,' Alvin said.

'He's living right on the top of Alto da Boa Vista. Almost out of this world.'

Mac was talking but thinking of that night when they had to run for their lives after violence broke out. He wondered whether Marisa had touched on this matter with Alvin. He was almost sure she hadn't, he knew her too well. He knew her much more than Alvin did. He wondered if Craig's uncle would mention it – even apologetically – when they went up. It was very likely. For this reason he was reserved about Alvin's going along with them.

He said to Marisa now, 'After the twenty fourth we'll just choose a Sunday eh, and we'll put that right. We'll see how the old man is getting on.'

'Alvin is going too?'

'You want to take him? If you want to take him it's all right.'

He tried to look at her warningly, but he could not do it well under the circumstances, and it did not get home to Marisa.

Alvin said, 'But I would like to go up too. I'd like to see any

Trinidadian here. You all reluctant for me to go?'

Mac said, 'No, you free – you welcome to come.'

'Because so far as I know, Craig was not in anything with Marisa.'

Mac was a little confused. He stuttered a little and then he said, 'Boy, you don't know how these old men are. I went up there to see Craig and Marisa went with me. The old man thought the world of Marisa, you know, and perhaps he thought this was a nice little partner for Craig. You don't know how these old men like to build hopes, boy.'

Alvin said bluntly, 'You ain't hiding anything from me?'

'Don't be an ass – excuse me Marisa. If this girl was in love with Craig she ain't 'fraid to say so. I never asked her her business. If you want to know, ask her.'

Marisa remained unruffled. Now she said to Mac, 'We must go up to see Uncle. Already we stay too long. I feel for him so much. And he will be so glad to see us. You can tell me when we can go, and we will go.'

'I'll tell you. It wouldn't be before the *passeata*, though.'

There was silence. Alvin was even more subdued now. He wanted to hear a few things about the *passeata* but he did not ask. Neither did Marisa ask, and Alvin realised that the word *passeata* had created a wall of silence between these two. He was jolted from his thoughts by Mac sliding off his stool.

Mac said, 'Don't move. Not a man move. But I have to go.'

Alvin said, 'Already?'

'Boy, I is a busy, busy man.' He paid for the drinks and he said, '*Caio*', and he was gone.

29

The very next time Mac saw Marisa he called her into his classroom and he said, 'I'm so sorry, Mar, I didn't realise you didn't tell Alvin about Craig.'

'That is all right. It is true that Craig and me did not reach anything.'

'I was worried. I thought you was vexed. By the way, you ever tell him about that night when he left?'

'You mean about the fighting? Nothing at all?'

'I thought so. The reason why I ain't so keen for him to go up is because Uncle might mention it.'

'I know.'

'You thought of it?'

'Yes. In the restaurant.'

He considered a little and he said, 'Blast it! We'll take him up. Else he'll feel so cut up.' Then he paused a little. 'Look, I wonder what is the position with Craig. He is fool enough to come back here you know. When he left – April? Look Mar, ain't it better for me to go up to Alto first, to see what's happening. Because that madman Craig could make a lot of trouble for you and Alvin. Anyway, after the *passeata* we'll talk about this.'

She remained looking at him.

He said, 'It's not my business but what's Alvin doing about you?'

She looked at him questioningly.

'I mean, he'll get married, or what? He's taking you over to Trinidad? Because he's only working here, for the Government. He'll have to go back.'

'He wants to stay in Brazil and he is seeing about it. We will get married.'

'Already? That lucky so-and-so! He'll look for a job here?'

'*I* am lucky.'

'What he'll do here when the trade office term – or what you call it – what he'll do here when that is finished?'

'He will teach English.'

'Oh, you two already plan that good! So you'll stay in this school?'

'He might open his own school.'

'Oh God, so you planning to leave me?'

'That will be hard.'

Mac said, 'Girl, life hard eh? Everything is frustration.'

'How is Ilka?'

He did not answer at first and then he said, 'She's okay. Why?'

'I am thinking of Linda. You will kill her.'

'Everything will kill Linda. That girl is too damn stupid. Look, even now – you see as I'm talking to you now, she's vexed like hell, you know.'

Marisa opened her mouth in alarm. Then she said, 'She is jealous of me, too?'

'*Claro.*'

'*Meu Deus!*'

'Anyway, I hope Alvin is good to you.'

'*Obrigada.* Thank you.'

'Seems a bit quick to talk about marriage.'

She did not answer.

'Of the lot of them I prefer you. I ain't making no fun.'

'But don't prefer me now. I have to prefer – how do you say *solteiro* in English?'

'Bachelor.'

'You are not a bachelor and you are very bad.'

'Okay. But still you are a lovely black girl and I don't want anybody to ill-treat you.'

'You keep talking about black but you married Linda who is white and you are loving Ilka who is white.'

'But I'm a man, and if a woman throws herself on me, what you want me to do? You know how Brazil is – the people I meet in my affairs are people like Linda and Ilka. And inside me girl,' his face hardened, 'deep inside me, I mean to take it out on them.'

'That's only an excuse.'

'You never take what I say, eh? You always arguing with me.'

'Because Mac you are a bad man.'

'Marisa, you know I can't understand you? You are a nice girl but you are a funny girl.' You against me, you against UNE, you against the *passeata,* you against everything revolutionary. And yet the revolution is for people like us – you and me.'

There was a look of pity on her face. She said, 'Mac, I now believe I am right that you are crazy. The revolution is for people like us? The *passeata* is for us?'

He laughed and shook his head. Then he laughed again. Now he said, 'What's your time there?'

'Ten minutes to six o'clock.'

'We had a nice long time talking. I'm glad you coming to school early every day now. Anyway I wanted to explain something but we ain't have time enough now. But Mar, come early again some time this week and I'll explain the whole set up to you. I mean the set up as Mac plan it. Take it easy.'

30

Round about the middle of the month so feverish with activity, Mac rushed in from *Centro* one noontime to hear Linda call out that someone was on the telephone to him. He took up the telephone and Ilka's voice said, 'I called for you now four times.'

Mac did not answer for an instant.

Ilka said, 'Where did you go?'

'I went to collect the things. The sticks. I don't want to say the word.'

'Dynamite.'

'Aha.'

'Good. Why you did not come last night?'

'I couldn't make it. I told you I mightn't come.'

Mac was uneasy. Linda was sitting right there, transferring notes and appointments into his diary from a little scrap pad. He knew that she was not understanding anything, and he saw that her suspicion was not aroused. But he did not want to trust to anything.

Ilka was complaining again that she had waited at Praça Quinze.

Mac said, 'But I just couldn't make it. Serious.'

'Who answered the telephone – she?'

'Aha.'

There was silence.

Mac said, 'Where you speaking from now?'

'Home. I am alone.'

'But you are not lonely?' He made a little fun.

She thought of the meaning of the word, then put it into Portuguese, and then she said: 'Yes, I am lonely. I am lonely for you.'

'Anyway, this is only a joke. I can't come now. I just this minute reached back.'

'For two hours last night I was at the Praça Quinze.'

'I can't leave that woman every night. Right now she is looking up at me every minute. I think she's beginning to suspect something. Good thing she is such an ass in English.'

Ilka chuckled. She said, 'Macky, I will see you tonight?'

'You won't see me before the big meeting tomorrow night. But I'll come early and we'll have a lot of time together.'

'You know well the address? I don't want to say it again on the telephone. Those *macacos* – how you say – monkeys, no?'

'Aha. I get it. I have the address all right. Anyway, I think I must go now. You know, this one here. I'll see you tomorrow. Wait in the usual place, eh?'

'*Bem*. She is still there?'

'Right here. Right here as I'm talking to you.'

'What is the English for *"vaca"*?'

'Take it easy.'

'But what is the English word for *"vaca"*?'

'Cow.'

'Blast that stupid cow.'

'Take it easy. You have too much temper.'

There was an angry silence on the other side.

Mac said, 'Look, I must go now. So cheerio.'

There was a sullen *"Ciao"*, as she put the telephone down.

31

A few Sundays before the *passeata* Marisa and Alvin were sitting in the praça when they noticed students gathering in front of the swings. When Marisa saw the blue and yellow scarves she said, 'It is the students of UNE. They are making a *comício* here.'

'What's that?'

'*Comício* is a political meeting.'

'But why here in Saens Pena?'

'I do not know why Saens Pena. Everywhere they are talking against the Government. It is because of the *passeata*.'

'But what about the police?'

'If they are big the police would come. Perhaps they are holding the meeting here because Saens Pena is far. Because it is away from the *Centro*.'

As they were talking the crowd was swelling in front of the swings. People were flocking into the praça from all directions.

Marisa said, 'I do not like this. I feel we should leave.'

'You are afraid of them?'

'There could be trouble with the police.'

Alvin looked at the excited, hysterical mass. He said, 'I wonder if these young fellers genuine.'

'They like excitement and trouble.'

'You think they could touch this Government?'

'I think, yes. Because the people are foolish. Look how they are rushing into the square to listen.'

Alvin said, 'Perhaps a few things really wrong with Brazil. Otherwise people wouldn't be so keen to condemn this Government.'

'There are many things wrong with the Brazil but also many things right. I love my Brazil.'

'Not you alone. I like this country too. Honestly.'

'The students are always talking about the poverty here. It is true that it is a poor country. It is true that there are *favelas*. All over America Latina there are *favelas*. There is also this about *racismo*.'

'Wouldn't you say that it exists?'

She hesitated. 'Yes, it exists. But it is because of rich and poor. Economic. And perhaps there are some bad people. But the Brazil is very good.'

Alvin was distracted. He was now looking towards the swings where the students were already beginning to speak. There were raised, high-pitched, voices and cries of '*Abaixo ditadura*'. People seemed to be pouring into the *praça* more than ever now and above the heads of the crowds banners were beginning to appear.

Alvin was getting nervous. He said, 'You want to get out of here? Let's go somewhere.'

'Where? Let me see. Do you want to see the Tijuca Forest? It is a nice place, like a garden botanico. It is on Alto da Boa Vista.'

The mention of Alto da Boa Vista brought Craig to mind, and he said, 'I think that's a bit far.' And then an idea came to his head. 'Why not take a bus ride down by me — down Copacabana.'

'No.'

'Why not?'

Suddenly there was a commotion in the crowd and they heard the shrill sound of a siren and three police cars pulled up at the far end of the *praça*. People scattered in all directions and shrieks pierced the air.

Alvin and Marisa scampered past the hedges and through the exit at the corner of Rua Saens Pena and Rua General Roca. They stood up on the pavement panting and excited. People were rushing across the road in front of the traffic.

Alvin was holding Marisa's hand and as he looked round he saw the white helmets heading for the top of the square. He held Marisa's hand and they dashed across the road to the pavement in front of the Banco da Guanabara. There was still a lot of confusion in the *praça* and Alvin could hear the thud of batons and the sound of broken glass behind him and people were running up the Rua Conde de Bonfim. He tried to get Marisa to trot to the bus stop on the Rua Conde de Bonfim. She was dead tired. He walked fast, tugging her along, but she felt very weak and she was shaking with fear. There were a lot of people about him. He reached the bus stop and he looked down the Rua Conde de Bonfim to see if there was any bus coming. As he looked he saw that the turmoil had spread to the other side of the road. His heart was thumping with fear. For once there were no buses in sight. He did not want to stand up so near to the praça. He said, 'Mari, try and walk. Let's hurry up to the next bus stop.' Marisa said nothing but she kept holding her hips and blowing. People were still fleeing from the praça up the Rua Conde de Bonfim but the action and turmoil still remained in the praça. He had his hands about Marisa and he was leading her up the hill but they were not moving very fast. He said to himself, 'Oh God, I only hope the police don't come up here.'

They reached the bus stop and they got on a bus going in the direction of Usina. Marisa was still trembling. They went to the back and sat down. He said, 'That wasn't so much. Don't make that worry you.'

She was blowing hard. '*Nossa Senhora*! We were lucky. You don't know what our police are like. If you don't run they beat you and if you run they beat you.'

'When they catch you. Well, they didn't catch us. Forget it.'

'We were lucky,' she repeated. Her heart was thumping so loud she could heart it.

'Where we heading for?'

The Usina.'

'And from there we going up to Floresta da Tijuca?'

'Oh, Alvin. Now it is best for me to go back home.'

'Home? You'll make that little thing make you want to go home?' Secretly, he too was frightened.

She remained silent, her head bowed. He threw his arms about her. After a few moments he said, 'Okay, let's get out at Usina and see how you feel.'

They stayed at Usina until it was dusk. Next to the bus station there was a cobbled stone courtyard with a long bench, and they sat down there. Marisa hardly spoke. When she saw lights beginning to appear in the hills about her she began to grow anxious to catch a bus for home.

She told Alvin and he said, 'Okay, you'll let me take you home?'

'Today, no.'

'You are still frightened?'

'No,' she smiled and looked at him. She appeared calmer now, but as one who had passed through a storm.

She said, 'You have not even the *visto* yet.'

'Oh, you mean the permission to stay in Brazil. They taking a hell of a long time. But have no fear. Everything will be all right.'

She looked a bit uncertain.

'In any case, if things don't work out I'll take you to Trinidad.'

She said, 'I am sure you will get the *visto*. I think now it is because they are all nervous about the *passeata*. But you will get it. I will go with you to see about it.'

'But even if I don't get it I must see your folks next week.'

'All right.'

'Anything new at the school?'

'It is what I told you already. Everything is political—'

'By the way, any news about Ilka?'

'Mac should know,' she smiled.

'You sure about this business with Mac? Because we ain't taking her back at the office.'

'Mr Wilkes said so?'

'*I* am saying so now. I want to bring you in.'

Marisa looked thoughtful and a little troubled. 'It is not better to wait until after the *passeata*? Then we can talk about it. It is only two weeks again.'

The bus sped along, and rushing in towards them now was Praça Saens Pena, brightly lit in the dusk. They both anxiously looked out to see if anything was still happening there, but the place looked quieter than on a normal Sunday. They got down at the bus stop in front of the Olinda Cinema.

On the pavement now she said, 'Tomorrow I will telephone for you. I go now.'

'You'll walk down there alone?'

'Yes. Tomorrow I will telephone.'

He gave her a kiss on the cheek and he said, 'Cheerio. See you.'

'*Ciao*.'

32

Just after classes on the Thursday night Ilka walked up the stairs of the Instituto MacDonald de Idiomas. On seeing her Mac was stunned. He did not know what to do.

'I came to see the school,' Ilka said.

Mac said, 'Oh. Okay. I'll show you round.'

Linda got up from the reception desk and she called Marisa. She asked Marisa who the girl was. Marisa said she did not know. Then Marisa went to Mac. She said, 'Mac, for the sake of peace it is better to get the Ilka out of here.'

Ilka said, 'No, get that woman out of here.' She stared fiercely at Linda.

Linda did not understand her words but she dashed into one of the classrooms and came out with a chair. She said to the girl, 'He wife, go.'

Mac stepped between the two women. He said, 'Ilka, look what you put me in.'

Ilka shouted, 'Okay, insult me in front of that cow.'

'She can't understand English — you know that.'

'You keep promising to me that you'll get rid of her. Get rid of her now.'

Marisa was holding back Linda who was struggling to get away. Linda was screaming at Mac to get Ilka out of her place.

Mac was so incensed he could not speak Portuguese. He cried, 'This is not your blasted place. You can't get her out of here. She stay here as long as I stay here.'

Not understanding what Mac said got Linda even more enraged. She screamed at Ilka: '*Vai*! Go! Go out!'

Suddenly she pushed Marisa away and rushed towards Ilka. Ilka stepped behind Mac and Mac with his left hand shielded her and with the right hand he chucked Linda away with such force that her body slammed against the reception desk. She rushed to where the broom was and as she grabbed it Mac side-stepped and caught hold of her arm and twisted it. He roared, 'Stop this bleddy nonsense. Stop it or I'll break your bleddy wrist.'

Linda remained quiet for a moment, grimacing with pain, but as soon as Mac relaxed his grip, she pushed him away and rushed at Ilka. There was no place to run and Ilka stood up and although she got some blows about the head she scratched Linda's face until the blood came. Mac now struggled to separate the two women, and as he pushed them apart Ilka got a grip on the neckline of Linda's dress and all but ripped it off her.

When Mac saw this he was so furious he chucked Ilka away. Ilka cried, 'You are trying to save your bloody *prostituta*. I will kill of you two.' She was at the open door of Marisa's classroom and she dashed in and picked up the vase of flowers from the table and flung it in the direction of Linda and Mac. It missed both and went crashing against the wall. There was water and petals and broken china all over the place.

Marisa cried, '*Men Deus*!' She had taken refuge behind the reception desk. When Linda saw the pieces of vase on the floor she burst out crying.

Mac said, 'Ilka, stop it now for Christ's sake.'

Ilka was as though she had run amok. She took up a chair but it was too ungainly and she could not do anything with it. As Mac moved towards her she picked up a wooden curio of Trinidad that Mac's father had sent him, and as she made to fling it at Linda, Mac said, 'Not that. Oh God, Ilka, not that!'

In the split second that Ilka paused Linda was upon her and let loose scratches and kicks and bites before Mac could do anything. Now Mac grabbed her left hand but as quick as lightning she whipped off her shoe from her right foot and cracked the heel on Ilka's head.

Mac was frantic. He jerked her away and in the same action crashed a right fist against her jaw. As she reeled, he caught her with a left punch, then he pounded her with another right fist which sent her in a heap to the floor.

He said, 'You too blasted bad. What the hell you think it is — you little bitch. I love this blasted woman more than you.'

Ilka came towards him now and they stood looking at Linda

lying on the floor. Linda was bleeding from the scratches on her face and also her jaw was swollen. She had fallen down heavily under the blows but now she raised herself to a half-sitting position.

She turned to Mac and panting heavily, she said, 'All right, Mac, she you love. Go, but always me *nesta escola*,' and she broke down crying.

Mac was holding Ilka's hand. He looked around him. He was still breathing hard. 'Where's Marisa,' he said.

Ilka had to catch her breath before answering. 'Oh — you mean — the other — girl?'

'Yes.'

'I do not know — when — she disappeared.'

'Let's go.'

'And leave her — there — on the floor?'

'Yes, let's go. Come on.'

They went down the stairs and across the street into Praça Saens Pena. They sat down on a bench at the far end of the praça, at a point from which they could see the lights of the school. Mac was watching to see if the lights would go off. He was worried and if the lights went off, that would calm him. He had hit Linda on the jaw with all the strength he had, and although she had talked afterwards, he felt that jaw was bound to be broken. If the lights went off he would be relieved.

He kept his eyes fixed on the windows. He had his arm about Ilka and as he relaxed a little he was conscious of her trembling.

'You all right?'

'Yes.'

'You cold? How you shaking so. Like you trembling?'

'I am afraid.'

'Afraid?' He took his eyes off the school to look at her. 'Girl, you ain't see a star pitch yet. You ain't see nothing yet. You afraid for that? You never see a man and a woman get away and break up? Girl, I am surprised at you. You in the thick of UNE and next week Monday we having a big demonstration.'

She was looking at him fixedly, and he put his eyes close to hers,' It's not a tea party you know, it's a demonstration. A political demonstration. If you 'fraid for a little scratch I don't know how you'll make out.'

She said, 'Do you think I am afraid of the blood? That is nothing. But the wife of yours is on the floor. Maybe she is not get up. If she die there, the police—'

Mac smiled, 'Ah, well, now you talking. You think I'll leave here if I don't see those lights go off? You joking! But Linda will get up. Although I hit her with everything. I know if we was still there she wouldn't get up – that's why I come in the square. I mean but if she's really injured we'll have to see what we could do.'

'You want to go back with her!' Ilka turned to him like a hawk.

'Never.'

'You sorry for her!'

He chuckled, 'I can't afford to be sorry for meself, this hour.'

After a little pause, she said, 'Mac, I wanted to ask you this: you and Linda, any *criancas?* Say no.'

'It's not a matter of just saying no. We ain't have any children, that's all.'

A wave of relief swept over her. She said, 'How long now you are married?'

'Just over a year.'

'And she is not – how you say – she is not *grávida?*

He laughed. 'Why you asking that silly question?'

'Because she looks so to me.'

'If she's having a baby that's her look out, but I don't know anything about that.'

'Perhaps I am wrong.'

'*Claro.* Wait, look!' The lights went off one by one. He said, 'She's got up.' He grinned like a child.

'Why you don't go over there and kiss her.'

He looked at her sharply. 'If I'd kill the bloody woman on the floor you'd feel good!'

Ilka was taken aback. After a moment she said, 'I know I am stupid, Mac, but it is because I like you.'

'I know.'

Both their eyes were turned to the school windows. After a while all the lights went off and the school was in total darkness. Mac felt relieved. He embraced Ilka. He said, 'Let's give her a little time to get out and then we'll go there.'

'That is why you beat her?'

'You know I want you. You know I love you.'

'*Bobagem.*' She lay her head against his shoulders. 'What is *bobagem* in English?'

'Nonsense.'

'You are full of nonsense,' she said.

They sat there for about half an hour afterwards. It was after eleven p.m. and there were now few people in the praça. Most of the buildings around Praça Saens Pena were in pitch blackness, excepting a few late-night cafes and restaurants. Mac's school was not too far from the junction of the Rua Conde de Bonfim with the Rua General Roca and the street lamp at the corner lightened the blackness around the pavement of his school. Mac's eyes were fixed on this area, straining to see if he could get a glimpse of Linda leaving the school. After a while he stopped talking. He saw a shadow move across the pavement and disappear into the darkness of the street. There were no vehicles passing to confirm that it was Linda but he was sure it could be nobody else. He turned to Ilka excitedly, 'She's gone.'

'You saw her?'

'I just saw her shadow cross the pavement.'

'And you going home with her?'

'Me? Look, it's either you or nobody in my life again.'

'But where you'll sleep tonight?'

'Right there in the school.'

'*Nossa Senhora!* Alone?'

'Alone. Just like that. Unless you want to come.'

'But Mac I have to go home.'

'Okay. Well, go home. I'll take you home.'

He already knew how much she wanted him and he knew that she did not want to lose him. He rubbed his head against hers, then he kissed her, and she leaned over onto his shoulder. He knew that she would go over to the school with him so he was gentle and he did not try to force her.

After a little while she said, 'It is getting late, Mac.'

'You want to go home? I'll take you home.'

'You are anxious for me to leave?'

'Not me. It's you. You said it's getting late. You look worried. I'm not.'

'I am not worried.'

'Well smile.'

She smiled in the dark.

Mac said, ' "The sunshine of your smiles". That's an English song.'

'But now it is not sunshine, it is night.'

'And it is late,' he mimicked her. Then he said, 'You going over?'

'Mac, you are silly.'

He said, 'Ilka, I want you to be brave. We are facing a big revolution, and as compared to that, your going over there with me is nothing. Anything could happen in that *passeata*. It's a *passeata* that could change the whole face of Brazil. You are in for that and yet you hedging over a little silly thing? You know I don't understand you? Sometimes you have to do what you really want to do — despite everything — once you really believe in it.'

Ilka just listened in silence.

'But it doesn't matter,' he said. 'My life is broken up already.'

'You are blaming me?' She looked up at him.

'I'm not blaming nobody.'

'I am not in fault. What do you want me to do?'

'Just stick by me.'

'You know I want to stay with you.'

'True?'

'Because if I don't stay I do not believe you will stay there alone. You will go back to her.'

'So you don't trust me?'

'No.'

He laughed.

'So do not do anything desperate and go back with her.'

'Not again.'

'You will be over there tonight?'

'Where — you mean the school?'

'*Claro.*'

'Yes. I'm going to sleep there.'

'Mac, first let me go home and I will come back and stay with you.'

33

Late the next week Alvin was surprised to hear Marisa's voice when he telephoned the Instituto MacWilliams de Idiomas.

'Oh, Mar, it's you? At last. What's happening, girl? You have me worried like anything.'

'I came out only today.'

'Yes, because all through the week I kept ringing and they told me you weren't out. What happen — you sick? What happened last Thursday?'

'When you can come down here?'

'I could come down tonight.'

'Okay, see you.' She put down the telephone.

Alvin reached Praça Saens Pena before nine o'clock and sat down near to the fountain waiting for Marisa. It was now past mid-June and the Brazilian winter had made the air chilly, and had made the trees a little bare of leaves. It was just a few days that Alvin had not seen the praça and yet it was already looking strange.

As soon as it was nine o'clock he got up and walked towards the other side of the fountain and stood up on the pavement. He had his eyes on the entrance of Mac's school.

Marisa soon came hurrying out with the hordes of students. She crossed the road very quickly and when they met they went back into the praça and sat down.

Alvin took her hand, 'How is it, Mar? Something happen? What happen?'

'On the telephone I could not speak.'

'I realised that.'

'You came to meet me the past Thursday?'

'I came to meet you but I didn't see you so I waited till ten o'clock and then I left.'

'The past Thursday Ilka came to the school.'

'Ilka?'

'There was such a fight. *Meu Deus.*'

'A fight? Between who? She and Linda?'

'At first it was with the Linda. The two of them was fighting and afterwards Mac gave Linda such *espancada.*'

'Jesu! You mean he brutalised Linda for Ilka?'

'Yes. I was sick. I had to go away.'

'But you were there when all this happened?'

'I was getting ready to go out to come and meet you when the Ilka come. And then there was the fighting. When I saw the blood on Linda I was so sick I forgot about you and about everything and went home. I cannot see blood.'

'But I mean, it's blood you talking about?'

'Ilka scratched her with the long *unhas*, fingernails, and she was bleeding. And her dress was tear. And afterwards Mac beat her. I wanted to call the police.'

Alvin was so shocked by the story he almost couldn't believe. He said, 'I didn't know Mac could be so inhuman.'

'I felt like calling the police. But when I got out there I thought I was going to faint. I went home.'

'And what happen to them. I mean, afterwards.'

'I only came back out this morning. It is now exactly a week. I do not know where is the Linda. Ilka is at the school. She is living with Mac. I cannot stay there.'

'Living with Mac? You serious? Heavens! And I don't know a thing. Since then I'm phoning every day. And I walked up and down in this General Roca a few nights ago. Looking for you. If I knew your house I would have come to find out, so help me! Anyway, how you feeling now?'

'All right, but I am still full of nerves.'

'I'm not surprised. When I phoned the school they kept telling me that you didn't come.'

'Who answered.'

'I don't know. It was a female voice. I thought it was Mac's wife.'

'You are right. That was Ilka. She is now the wife of Mac,' she said. She gave a sour smile.

'That was Ilka, really? Then she was disguising her voice.'

'I do not know but I think it must be the Ilka. The students say she was there since the past Friday. She is now in the reception in place of the Linda.'

'And how she was?'

'I do not like her. She did not say one word to me.'

'But why you went back?'

'I do not want to go back now.'

'I should think so. You saw Mac?'

'Yes.'

'He told you anything?'

'He said he thought I left but he was glad I came back.'

'The cheek! That's all?'

'We did not have much time to talk and afterwards I hurried out to meet you.'

'Mac is a dirty dog!'

'It is not Mac, it is the Ilka.'

'Heavens! That's a pair, eh? Those bastards.'

'You hear yet about the *visto* – to stay?'

'Girl, not yet. But I'm not worried about that now. That school is no place for you. Don't bother to go back there.'

'I do not tell Mac anything.'

'You don't have to tell him a single thing. Just don't go back. Wilkes was holding on to Ilka's job, thinking she was sick. I didn't want to say anything about those two – because of what you told me, but now—'

'Do not tell him what happened, please.'

'But I'll have to let him know she ain't coming back. And I'll tell him about you.'

'I would prefer after the *passeata* – it's just Monday.'

'You afraid for the *passeata* too?'

'No, I am not afraid about the *passeata*, but afterwards Mac is going to the Alto da Boa Vista with us, and—'

'Not with me. You mean you still thinking of going up there with him?'

'But I must see the old man. I just must. It was bad of us not to go to see him before this time.'

'In any case I don't see why you have to go. I don't see why you have to go to see Craig's uncle, anyway. But if you have to go, you can't go by yourself?'

Marisa felt pained. She said, 'Alvin, Mac is bad and Mac is crazy, but he was very nice to me. And since I will not stay at his school it might be the last time we will meet. I must go up to the Alto with him.'

'Well, in that case it sounds reasonable. Go up then,' Alvin said.

There were many people about in the praça, and there were many children, with their nursemaids, at the playground end. Some of the children were on the swings. Alvin and Marisa sat secluded, in pensive mood. They were talking only now and then.

34

On Sunday, with only hours between, the fear and fever of the *passeata* gripped Rio de Janeiro. The city was tense and waiting. Students were already pouring in from all the states and the place was beginning to take on the look of Carnival time.

On the Avenida Rio Branco, in the centre of the town, slogan-shouting students were already beginning to throng the Universidade Pacheco. At the same time, truck-loads of armed police were beginning to take up their positions around the university compound.

At the university itself, the final meeting of the leaders of the *passeata* had just ended.

Now, in the first hour of the morning, Mac and Ilka alighted from a bus in front of the Olinda Cinema in Saens Pena. They walked right across the praça to the fountain, then crossed the Rua Conde de Bonfim. As they turned into the entrance of the Instituto MacDonald de Idiomas, something shuffled in the shadows and they saw that it was a policeman. They went on up the stairs. After they got inside and bolted the door, Mac said, 'So they starting to follow us!'

Ilka said nothing. She was wearing her Che Guevara shirt – with big pockets on the front and sides – and trousers to match, and her face looked pale without makeup. Her blonde hair was tied in a great knot behind her head.

She had sat down in a chair and now she went and opened one of the windows and looked out. After a moment she shut the window and mumbled something which Mac did not understand.

'What's that?'

'I was just cursing those pigs in German.'

'But you good man. I never hear you talk German.'

She said nothing.

'And you know I always think of you as Spanish? I don't know why. In fact, I always think of you as Eva Peron. A real revolutionary. And she looked like you, too – only smaller.'

'*Si*.'

'Oh, you could talk Spanish.'

'But oh yes,' she looked at him.

'You are a real linguist. You could talk Spanish, Portuguese, English and German.'

'And French.'

'And *French*. But girl you is a wall.'

He was sitting on one of the chairs in the reception room. Although he was talking light-heartedly he was pondering on the policeman. Then he made some effort to shift his thoughts from the policeman and he looked at Ilka. He thought, what a girl, what a fighter. And she couldn't care less what those damn UNE racialists have to say.

He said, 'You tired?' She was nodding on herself on the chair.

His voice jolted her a bit. She said, '*Nossa*! I will never wake up.'

He sat up. 'What's that? Girl, you mad? Don't make those kinds of joke.'

She laughed.

He said, 'Anyway. I might have to wake you up. You don't think you should go to sleep now?'

'Yes.'

She remained sitting, overcome with tiredness, then she got up eventually and she went into the little room where the audio-visual teaching equipment had been. The equipment was now in the room where Mac had held his English conversation classes, and now English conversation was held in the reception room. The reception room was cluttered with chairs.

Now that Ilka had gone into their little bedroom Mac went to the window and looked down. From the line of the building with the pavement he could just see the rim of the policeman's blue helmet. Oh God, Mac boy, he thought. Oh God, if you only had something weighing a ton, eh, and he was bareheaded! He unbuttoned his shirt and he put his hand deep down by his navel and he felt the butt of his revolver. It was loaded, and the point was stuck between his trousers and his thighs.

There was no question of his using it. He had only had a sudden fit of rage, on seeing the policeman below, and he had thought of killing him, but he had no intention of being so rash as to use his pistol. But he would have dearly liked to finish off a policeman. He was thinking, Oh God, in this *passeata*, if one of them only make a slip up—'

'Macky,' Ilka called.

'Aha.'

She didn't say anything else and he knew she was calling him in to bed. He looked at his watch, which was showing a few minutes to two o'clock. He remained at the open window looking at Praça Saens Pena in darkness, and taking in a little more fresh air. Then he closed the window and went inside. He said to her, 'You sleeping already?'

'No.'

'You have to be up in a few hours.'

'I will be up long before you.'

As he changed into his pyjamas he looked at her lying there as if she were dead. The bed was two couches jammed side by side.

'Girl, you look as tired as me.'

She turned over to one side. All but her head was under the sheet.

'Ilka.'

Imitating him, she answered, 'Aha.'

'The meeting was a little long.'

'But *impressionante*.'

'Okay. I'm glad you talking Portuguese, because we mustn't talk English tomorrow.'

'You will forget.'

'Me? Never.'

'You say the meeting was long?'

'I find it so. I don't like too much talking. You see this?' He pointed to the revolver on a chair, 'If it comes to it, this will talk for me.'

'Try not to make use of it.' She looked at him.

'I'll try not to and I only hope those *macacos* don't force me to.'

'But take it easy.'

'What? I could take it easy in this fascist country?'

'It is a lot of them, Mac. And I want you.'

He said nothing.

She remembered the book by Erich Remarque, *A Time to Love and a Time to Die*. The title fitted neatly into her thoughts.

She said, 'Those *macacos*. Sometimes I am afraid of them.'

'What?'

'They have guns. Plenty guns.'

'Well at least it will be gun against gun. Mac 'fraid no man.'

She looked at him with quiet admiration. Really, she was not afraid of the soldiers and the police. She was only afraid because of Mac – because she was afraid to lose him. But now, for saying this, she loved him even more. At last she had got a companion with more fire than herself. All the boys she had had, all the boys she had known, were only full of talk. All the fire they had was for something else. They would not be seen with a gun – in fact, if they heard one fire they would scamper off. But they blabbered of revolution, they wanted to change the country! Thank goodness, now she had a man like Mac. She would stick with him through calm and through raging storm. He was a true revolutionary; he was hot-blooded and afraid of no man. And like herself he was not even Brazilian!

Her thoughts raced on like this in the silence and at length, seeing Mac was still sitting up, she said, 'The lights, Mac. Take it off. Come on to bed. Let us sleep.'

'You calling this a bed?' he laughed.

He put the revolver down carefully on the chair and he switched off the lights. Then he slipped under the sheets and tried to sleep.

35

Before dawn cleared on Monday morning the streets of *Centro* were already teeming with people. Train loads and bus loads of students were coming in from all directions, and the students from the other boroughs were massing in the town.

By eight o'clock in the morning this central area of Rio de Janeiro was a seething mass. And mingling with the crowds everywhere were the blue and black uniforms of the police. The students were gathering in front of the Universidade Pacheco, on the Avenida Rio Branco, and huge, troop-carrying lorries had already arrived in the vicinity. The soldiers were armed and in battle dress, ready for action. Some of them moved on the pavement with the police, while the rest sat on the troop-carriers, watching. At intervals, as the students surged along the Avenida Rio Branco, packed troop-carriers raced down the street with sirens screaming, and came to a halt outside the university.

By the time the clock moved on to nine, the centre of the city was a jam-session of people. The city's main street, the Avenida Rio Branco, was now so packed with students that now no vehicle – not even army troop-carriers, could move along it. The entire street, from the waterfront where it began to the Praia do Flamengo where it ended, was a solid block of people, mainly students. And not too far from the university, where the city's principal street – the Avenida Presidente Vargas – intersected the Avenida Rio Branco, the crowd on either side was like a raging sea.

The police and soldiers mingling with the crowd were in fact very nervous. The crowd, bristling, had already taken up the students' chant of '*Abaixo Ditadura*'. But the police did nothing but jostle and mingle with the people.

In the street, just before the university, were mounted policemen. They were greatly agitating their horses but they could not keep the crowds off the roadway. They used loudspeakers calling on the students to clear the streets, and more than once they charged the crowds, but they could not get the area clear.

From the university itself, the leaders of the *passeata* also used loudspeakers, and they too were trying to control the crowds. They had not expected such a massive turnout of supporters and they feared police brutality. As the mounted police charged and shouted the crowd heaved like an angry sea.

Ilka stood on the balcony at the front of the university and looked down at the crowd. There were many other student leaders around her on the balcony. She and Mac had arrived in the very early hours of the morning. In fact, Ilka had not slept at all. Now she was dressed in a red bodice and a pair of blue dungaree trousers and soft crepe-soled shoes. Her hair was gathered together tightly and knotted at the top of her head.

She was among the four or five leaders who were trying to marshal the crowds into an orderly manner and trying to get them to start forming up for the *passeata*. She was shouting instructions at the top of her voice, and now when she felt she was getting hoarse she gave up the loudspeaker and went upstairs to meet Mac.

Mac, too, was wearing a pair of blue dungarees, and he was wearing a university pullover on top of an old shirt. He was looking out of one of the windows over the Avenida Rio Branco, and he was watching how some mounted policemen were charging a section of students, and his heart burned him. He felt inflamed. He wished he were in that crowd to blurt out a few cutting words. He wanted to spit on the mounted policeman but there was the mass of people below who might get it. He looked at the turning, twisting figures down below and he felt revulsion not only for them in themselves but for the horses. He watched the policemen and said, 'You blasted stooges you – we'll do for you all today.' The students beside him turned and looked at him – for they did not know he spoke English. They did not understand what he said.

He was still looking down on the blue and black uniforms and on the helmets of the policemen and soldiers. Although he felt enraged, he thought really it would be better for him not to be too near to them today. But he did not want to be too far from them either. He put his hand below his shirt and felt the metal cold against his waist. He knew it was still there, of course, but he had wanted to touch the hardness of it. It gave him a thrill just to feel it there. He had to be careful how he touched it for it was loaded. He put his hand from below and he felt the butt and it was all right. He breathed out a big sigh. Then he jumped as he felt the hand on his shoulder.

Ilka grinned.

'Oh God, girl, it's you? You make me jump.'

'You are nervous? Today you must be cool in the head.'

'You right. What about this march. When they starting? It's time for the bleddy *passeata* to leave.'

'Bloody *passeata*? You wish for blood here?' She was trying to make fun to calm her nerves. She was feeling all filled up and her heart was racing.

He was looking down into the street below. He said, 'Bloody is just a term. We leaving just now?'

'Yes, we will begin very soon now. Look at the main entrance where it is forming up. Things will begin now. Look over there where Vladimir is. We will soon be on the street.'

She stopped and listened to the loudspeaker. It was still calling for an orderly line-up of the marchers. Below, as far as the eye could see, there were people. She turned and said, 'Macky, today we do not speak the English. The students will think we are American. It is dangerous. For the students it is bad to be American.'

Mac was excited and nervous. He said, 'So only the blasted Americans speak English? In any case, why it's bad to be American. Look, look – they forming up now. What you doing – you going down now?'

He heard the voice over the loudspeaker calling the officials together. Ilka paused beside him. She said, 'Macky, don't move, please. Do not leave here. I will go down to see Vladimir, but I will come back.'

She went on talking, and midway in her conversation she switched to Portuguese. It was not because she knew that English was dangerous but because she was overcome with emotion and could speak only Portuguese now. After a few more moments she left to go down the stairs.

She felt weak and held on to the rails. As she got near to the balcony where the *passeata* officials were she could see the crowd pouring into the Avenida Rio Branco. It looked like a river breaking its banks, with nothing being able to withstand that tide – not even the policemen. The crowd surged and the policemen lined the pavement on the far side.

Ilka had never seen such a huge crowd as this. She tried to squeeze through the throng in the university hall to get to the *passeata* officials. The loudspeaker was still calling on the students to take to the streets. As Ilka squeezed through the flowing mass, revolutionary songs broke out across the street and banners took to the air. When Ilka reached Vladimir Palmyra and the other officials she was too overcome to talk.

Mac waited for Ilka until almost everyone had gone down stairs and he grew impatient and angry. He could not believe that she was so carried away that she had forgotten him. But there was no sign of her. He wanted to go downstairs and join the mass of people moving out into the street but he knew that if he shifted from where he was he and Ilka would never find each other again until everything was over. He turned back towards the window and looked downstairs. On the Avenida Rio Branco there was a solid mass of humanity stretching as far as he could see. Some sections of the crowd were beginning to sing revolutionary songs, and banners were taking the air.

He said to himself, 'Look I going down, you hear! Oh God!' He left the window and joined the students streaming down the stairs. A student who had been standing beside him, left too. Mac was in a hurry and he pushed and squeezed to make way. He passed quite near to Ilka who was going up to meet him.

Long before the demonstration cleared the university, Rio de Janeiro's whole downtown area was jammed with people. The Avenida Rio Branco was a seething mass. People, old and young, students and non-students filled the streets and pavements and side streets of the *avenida* as the demonstrators made their way towards the Avenida Presidente Vargas. When the procession reached the Avenida Presidente Vargas it wormed its way along one side of the church Candelária and headed for the nearby square – Praça Quinze de Novembro.

As the procession moved, the city seemed bathed in a sea of banners. The police followed in lorries, vans, and on foot, with the chief on horse back – and all the way they were jeered and insulted by the crowd. They were so tense they kept their hands on their firearms.

The head of the police contingent was riled and nervous. He had personally pressed for the banning of the *passeata,* declaring it to be communist, but the authorities had not listened to him. They had wanted to show how democratic Brazil was. Now, with '*Abaixo Ditadura*' on the lips of the masses and with pictures of the Cuban guerilla Che Guevara on most of the banners, he wondered how the authorities would feel. But it was hardly a matter of how they felt. Authorities or no authorities, Brazil was his country, and his country was in revolution. And it was his duty to put down the revolution.

He had galloped just beyond Candelária, and now he turned his horse round to look at the advancing tide. He could not even see the junction of the Avenida Rio Branco and Presidente Vargas – so dense was the crowd. The head of the procession advanced towards him and the praça was at his back.

This was by far the greatest crowd he had ever had to deal with and though he felt angry and defiant there was a little voice inside him which told him to be careful. He had called up his men, and now when he saw behind him the flank of foot and mounted policemen, and when he saw the soldiers in battle dress everywhere, he felt capable and secure.

Suddenly his eyes caught a dark ring in the sky. He was looking towards the Avenida Presidente Vargas, and this was above it, in the distance far away. He winced. He did not like this sign. Although deep down inside him he had felt to mow down this crowd, which he thought of as lunatic, he was not happy to see crows circling in the sky. He told himself that if this was to be a bloody day, he had already done all in his power to prevent it.

The advancing crowd had now reached him and he heard all sorts of insults unleashed at him. He made his horse back slowly before them, in the direction of the praça. The insults stung, but he could not answer them verbally, but there was one answer for them. People were swelling around him now and his horse became jumpy and there were some trying to scare it. He turned the horse round in a circle, pressing people back. Now he was quite deep in the torrent of people and he decided to bring his horse a little nearer to the rest of the policemen. As he turned around and saw the praça a thought struck him and his head became hot. If the students continued beyond Praça Quinze they were soon going to come to the American Embassy, and there was bound to be trouble. Perhaps there was where they were heading for! He had heard anti-American slogans and it only now occurred to him what the marchers' intentions might be. He did not like it. He knew UNE to be very hostile to the Americans. If this massive crowd of so-called revolutionaries were to pass in front of the American Embassy – if even it was only passing – there was bound to be trouble. He could not let this happen. He blew his whistle and signalled to all the policemen to come up. He turned round to make for the square.

As he pulled the bridle the horse reared, and panic-stricken people dived out of the way. Some came close to being trampled. At this, someone screamed a curse at him, and he wheeled around, bristling. He had his baton already raised and he scanned the section of the crowd below him to see who had called him the son of a whore. He was panting with rage and now he turned his horse round from side to side not caring whether anybody got trampled. The woman's voice that cried '*Filho da Puta*' rang against his mind and he would crack her skull if she would only show herself. Now there was only the muffled rumble and blank faces below him and he turned again to ride off. As he turned, about two or three voices screamed out, '*Filho da puta!*'

As the demonstrators came out of the Avenida Rio Branco, seeing that there were no policemen about, they ran amok among the big stores, breaking the glass show-windows and looting. The students wrote revolutionary slogans on the closed doors, and they daubed red paint freely not only on the shop doors but on walls and statues in their paths.

Now at this junction of the two great avenidas people were packed close. It looked as if the whole of Rio de Janeiro was on the streets. But still there were people moving to *Centro* from all directions. The singing of revolutionary songs and the mass of colour made it look like Carnival. Yet, even at that stage the tail of the procession had not been able to clear the university.

The police chief, Pedro, was now at the head of the procession. When it eased past Praça Quinze de Novembro he gave another

blast on his whistle and this time he signalled to the *passeata* leaders
that the *passeata* must stop. The foot and mounted policemen jostled
up to the front with their weapons at the ready.

There was consternation among the students. Hastily, one of
the organisers took a loudspeaker and announced that the *passeata*
was being stopped by the police, and he appealed for calm. A
threatening roar went up and for the moment it looked certain that
there would be a clash between the demonstrators and the police.
But amidst the shouts and insults the *passeata* came to a halt.

There was a moment of great tension. The singing in front
stopped. And now the cry, as if in unison, went up: '*Abaixo ditadura!*
Abaixo ditadurar!'

Mac was in this section of the crowd and he shouted this slogan
until his voice was hoarse and he felt his throat burning and dry. He
was so excited that he confused his Portuguese and at moments he
cried: 'Down with dictatorship.'

A few of the policemen had noticed this and had been watching
him. They had been informed of American communists infiltrating
UNE but to them this was the first living proof. They decided to trail
him.

At first, the *passeata* had stopped completely, but now pressure
from behind – pressure coming from right back, even from people
just leaving the university – caused it to creep forward a little, pressing
back the police.

The police got incensed. They blared a warning on the
loudspeaker that if the march did not stop they would fire. The
students at the front desperately tried to stop. But as they stumbled
forward they faced the police with defiance.

As the police raised their guns many dropped their banners and
grabbed up stones, and just then Mac went to bend down he saw a
group of policemen looking at him. He slid his right hand to his hip
and felt the hardness of his revolver. He did not pick up the stone,
then.

At this time the police chief rode up calling on the demonstrators
to disperse. They remained firm. He cast his eyes around. Praça
Quinze itself and the streets around it seethed with people. The police
chief was not afraid, but he felt he would like to get this sort of
crowd broken up as soon as possible. He felt since he had got it to

stop he could get it to disperse. Over the loudspeaker he again called on the people to go home. But the crowd grew more and more hostile. When the police chief gave a command and rode back a few paces, the first of the tear-gas cannisters burst into the air.

The students backed away in confusion and there was a roar of '*Abaixo ditadura*,' as the wind blew the tear-gas across the crowd. There was hysterical coughing and there were people running in all directions, their hands on their eyes. Suddenly a shower of stones rained on the police. Some of the policemen rushed at the students and the students took refuge behind the pillars and statues in the square. Stones continued to rain on the police and now these stones were coming from all sections of the crowd. The police chief fired into the air. This did not stop the students from running amok, attacking the police with stones and breaking the windscreens of police vehicles. Some of the policemen had to take cover behind vehicles and trees.

Now there was more of the shattering sound of tear-gas, and the gas itself, like a cloud, enveloped the praça. In a short while most of the demonstrators had fled the praça, overcome by the gas, and the policemen, with gas-masks, pursued them, using their batons freely. Some of the young women trapped by the gas in the middle of the praça remained there covering their faces with their clothes. The police collected them into vans.

After about ten minutes Praça Quinze itself was nearly empty but students continued to attack the police. Now they were attacking from the side streets of the praça, be-hind the houses. Every now and again they threw stones at the police, and when the policemen rushed at them they quickly dispersed. This enraged the police. They were determined to dislodge these demonstrators. Their vans slowly became filled up with badly beaten youths.

The clashes between the students and the police around Praça Quinze went on well into the morning. Far from the students being dislodged from the side streets and among the houses, there seemed to be a growing concentration of students on all sides, behind the houses. And still the stones came. Most of the stones were coming from a heap put aside for roadworks in one of the back streets, and these stones were being distributed to the students, who were pelting from various points.

The policemen knew there was a heap of stones somewhere but did not know exactly where it was. The stones continued to keep the police at bay. They injured some of the policemen themselves, while they did some damage to police equipment, police vehicles, street lights, and even some of the glass windows of the surrounding houses.

The occupants of the buildings around the square were terrified. Also they were in anguish because of the tear-gas, but they were afraid to flee their homes because of the armed police outside. The air of the praça lay heavily blue with the gas. But the determined students stuck to the conflict. Sometimes they took refuge in the houses round the praça and when the police arrived they could not tell who were occupants and who were not.

Mac was standing with about two or three others at the heap of stones. There was a young girl down the lane looking out for police, and Mac was busily supplying stones so that the revolutionaries could keep up the barrage and force the police out of the praça. He wanted so much to humiliate the police; he wanted so much to force them into a defeat.

One of the policemen was walking stealthily among the houses in the back streets when suddenly his heart jumped. He spotted a girl from afar, and hiding and following her movements he saw the man by the heap of stones. He was heavily armed. He walked across three cross streets and when he reached where he thought he had seen the girl there was no sign of her and he knew that he had lost himself. He tried to find his bearings by looking for the 'smoky' tear-gas air of the praça, but by now the wind had blown the smokiness all over the place. He came out into a side street opening on the praça but he saw nothing. The students were massed on the other side but he could swear he had seen a group in this street.

As he was on the point of turning back a man passed across his view. He dashed to a corner of the house, saw the man again, and with his baton raised, advanced. Mac heard the heavy boots and looked back. Now he rushed for stones from the heap but the policeman was almost upon him. He swung back and grabbed and with the same action he shied a stone. This cowed the policeman and he stopped in his tracks. They were facing each other now, a little distance apart. Mac had grabbed another stone and now the policeman swayed and jumped, trying to make Mac miss with it, but as he jumped the stone caught him squarely on the ribs and knocked the baton out of his hand. Blood soaked the policeman's shirt. Mac swung round to the stone heap to get a stone to knock down the policeman finally, but by the time he straightened up the policeman had pulled his revolver.

They were close to each other and the policeman was aiming at his head. Mac cried, 'You'll kill a black man like yourself?' He was shaking with fear. 'You'll kill a black man because he fighting for freedom?'

The policeman stayed his finger on the trigger, amazed. He was expecting to hear blabbering in Portuguese but now it was English that poured out.

The policeman growled, 'You Americano *porque* the fighting *em* Brazil?'

Mac realised that he had made the mistake of speaking English. Now with the revolver pointed at his head he could not think in Portuguese at all. He stuttered, and as he stuttered the hand slid to his waist and the policeman saw what he was reaching for. He saw the shape of the black butt underneath the shirt. He pulled the trigger and Mac fell.

It was not yet eleven o'clock in the morning when the news of the killing spread to the students. The *passeata* had already broken up but the students were grouping and holding *comicios* all over the city. When they heard that a student was killed they were enraged. They screamed *'Abaixo ditadura!'* at the police and wherever policemen were absent they broke the glass windows of the big shops, destroyed street lamps, and plastered anti-Government slogans all over the city.

In *Centro* itself all that remained to the police was to get rid of the hundreds of demonstrators that had sought refuge in the church of Candelária. They did not want to enter the church but they formed a ring around it, and there were soldiers standing at the entrance with bayonets fixed.

The sight of bared bayonets riled the students and there was a steady chorus of *'Abaixo ditadura!'* The police and soldiers did not want to cause any desecration of the church and they just stood up waiting patiently. The students inside the church did not defile or disrespect anything. They stood up shouting their slogans, and some prayed.

There was only one casualty around Candelária. That was Ilka. Ilka, after hearing of Mac's death, had run amok after the police, and bayonets had chased her into Candelária, and she had collapsed on the steps. Now there was a group of policemen around her and they had been waiting a little time for an ambulance to take her away.

The students inside Candelária did not surrender and when it was three o'clock the police fired tear-gas into the church.

As the students rushed out they met a flurry of batons and hundreds of them were arrested and driven away to detention. Then *Centro* was as quiet as the grave.

After Ilka had received first aid at Candeléria she had been taken to police headquarters where she was interrogated but was not put into the cells. The young officer who questioned her wanted to set her free because she was attractive and because she was the one who was bereaved by today's clashes – which meant that she had no husband.

He had looked at her all the time and she had looked back at him coldly. After the interrogation he had asked her if he could take her home and as she did not answer he had left her on the steps and gone around to the back to get a police van. All the time he was acting with seriousness of face so that his colleagues would not suspect anything.

He fetched her from the steps and drove off towards Praça Saens Pena. As soon as he drove off his voice softened and he spoke now in a friendly intimate way. But not once did she open her mouth and not once did she look at him. When they arrived at the Instituto MacWilliams de Idiomas he held her hands and asked if he could take her upstairs. She jerked away her hand angrily, opened the door of the van, and got out. It was the first violent action she had made since she had collapsed on the steps of Candelária. She did not glance at the officer – nor at the praça – which looked desolate in the approaching dusk. She walked up the stairs weakly. The key of the apartment was in the back pocket of her dungaree, but she was not thinking of the key very much. It would not have mattered to her if the key had been with Mac, as it usually was. Or if they had kept it at police headquarters. She put her hand in her back pocket and took out the key. She opened the door and she went to the room where they had slept. Then she threw herself on the bed and burst out crying.

36

August had already come in, when, sitting at Marisa's home one day, Alvin asked, 'Mari, have you ever heard anything about Mac and Ilka?'

'Never. After the *passeata,* never.'

'That's funny, eh? And you never went back upstairs in that Instituto?'

'*Clara.* I went there about one month after. I did not tell you? I went there hoping to meet Mac or to find out something. But no one was there.'

'Look how the place is a restaurant now, eh? *O Mundozinho.*'

'Yes.' She was contemplating just that. Life was quick with its changes. Her heart pained her.

Alvin said, 'They must have gone to some other state or something. I don't know. You always said Mac was crazy.'

Marisa tried to smile, although inside her she felt herself near to tears. She bit her teeth.

Alvin said, 'But he still had some good points. I often wonder about him.'

They were sitting in the verandah and Marisa had her head turned towards the road.

Alvin said, 'You well quiet. What you thinking of?'

'I am looking to see if my mother is coming.'

Alvin smiled to himself.. They never feel safe without their mothers, he thought.

He said, 'It's funny how I should just stay so and think about the *passeata.*'

'What made you think about it?'

'It was that scrawl on the Olinda Cinema. You know the students scrawled up on everything? It's that big red scrawl: "UNE CONTINUA".'

'Aha,' she said, which put Mac in her thoughts again.

Alvin said, 'That *passeata* was something. It must have shaken everybody in Rio.'

'And what about the Uncle up there on the Alto – you think it shaken him too?'

'Oh, you mean Craig's uncle? What about him?'

'I don't know.'

'Let's go up to see him. I mean, he's a Trinidadian; I feel I should go up to see him.'

'Yes,' she said, 'We can go up.'

A thought came to her that going up there she might be able to find out something about Mac. But then she knew Mac would not go up there without her. Mac could not be in Rio. He must be somewhere far, far. 'It is the Ilka,' she told herself, and her heart bled. She was going to marry Alvin but she would never forget Mac, nor his madness and all that went with it – not even the teeming streets.

Michael Anthony was living in Rio de Janeiro when the student riots of 1969 occurred, and has woven his fictional story into events which he himself observed.

Born in Mayaro, Trinidad, he moved to England as a very young man and lived there for many years. It was in England that his first three novels were written: The Games Were Coming, The Year in San Fernando and Green Days by the River. In England he married (his wife, too, is Trinidadian) and three of his children were born. The youngest was born in Rio. In 1970 he decided to take his family home to Trinidad, where they have lived since then.

Printed in the United States
213001BV00002B/1/A

9 789766 372880